My Stepfather Sold Me to Save His Farm

Joanna Grayson

PublishAmerica
Baltimore

ISBN: 1-60813-829-1
PUBLISHED BY PUBLISHAMERICA, LLLP
www.publishamerica.com
Baltimore

Printed in the United States of America

This book is dedicated to my loving son;
Stephen Paul Johnson
Who has always been my true inspiration!
June 04, 1979—March 27, 1999

I would like to thank my family for always being supportive of this book.

I owe a special thanks to
My husband Gary, my daughter Marie,
my sisters Linda and Cindy
For their extra help and support!

My life was about to go through a life shattering change. I would lose both parents, fall in love with my step brother and sold to save my step fathers farm.

My father did not live with my mother and me; he would show up several times a year and spend a couple of days. When he was around we would have the best time together.

When I was eight, my mother remarried and we had to move to the farm where my step father and step brother lived. They had a lot of farm hands to help them run it. My step brother was four years older than I and so very nice to my mother and me.

On the farm the summers were always so hot and the winters were so very cold. We were so far away from everyone and everything. My step brother and I became very close. We became quite the little family; so I thought!

In the summer, we would stay at the lake as often as possible. My stepfather's house didn't have air conditioning however, did have window and ceiling fans to cool us off. We went barefoot most of the time and wore mostly shorts and tank tops. We spent most of our days fishing, riding horses and swimming when we weren't doing our chores!

In the winter the snow got so high it would almost touch the bottom of my bedroom window which was on the second floor. We only had one fireplace which was in the living room. We had a lot of thick covers on our bed and mom would make us wear long johns under our pajamas. Some winters would get so bad with the ice and winds we would lose some of the farm animals. My step father had to make regular trips into town, bad weather or not and there were times he would get stuck there for the night. I would worry about my mother because she would get sick a lot during the winter.

I must say; never in my wildest dreams did I ever think I would be rented out, and sold like live stock.

CHAPTER ONE

We lived in Las Vegas where my mother at eighteen became a show girl at one of the casinos. My mom said back then, that was about the best paying job you could get. She started seeing one of the owners of the club and she became pregnant with me. She and my dad were married in the hospital right before I was born. My dad wanted me to have his name even though they never lived together. My dad didn't want my mom to go back to work in the casino. He said that was no place for a child to grow up. He wanted me to have a normal childhood, so he opened a store and named it M&M Supplies. He named the store after my mom and himself. They divorced shortly after I was born and in the divorce my dad signed the store over to my mom. They both always told me how much they loved me, but I never heard them tell each other that.

My mom met all kinds of guys in her store and she went out with a few of them. One day she started seeing a man; his name was Brad. Mom said he was from Wisconsin and he owned a farm there. Brad was always very nice to me, and had a son named Curtis. They would come and stay off and on when school was out. Curtis was very nice to me and I liked them both. My mom and Brad started talking to us one night. They had been dating for three years and they were talking about getting married. They wanted to know how we felt about it. Curtis and I had no problem with it, we all got along fine. But there is a catch my mother said, "If we do get married, we will have to move into Brad's house." I didn't mind them getting married but I didn't want to leave my home, my friends or my real dad.

Even though my dad didn't live with us he would come visit me several times through out the year. My mom said she would also have to sell the store and our home. I became very angry about that and reminded her that my daddy bought her that for us and I didn't want to leave. We lived in town and I could stay at the store as much as I wanted. Brad lived on a farm in a different town, in a different state. I cried myself to sleep that night knowing no matter what I said or did we would have to leave.

Brad told us that his wife died when Curtis was only three months old. A bad summer storm had hit and she put Curtis in the playpen while she ran outside to get the clothes off the line. As she was running to get back into the house a tree fell on her, by the time they found her, she was already gone. The doctor told Brad she had internal bleeding and even if he had found her earlier she still would not have made it. Curtis didn't know what it was like to have a real mom and his dad had never remarried. My mom told me to be a good girl because this family really needed us. I did feel sorry for Curtis, I had a mom and somewhat of a dad, but Curtis only had a dad.

Brad had decided that my mom and I should go ahead and move to the farm so we could get settled in before the wedding. We took a plane to Wisconsin and Brad was waiting at the airport for us when we arrived. Two of Brad's farm hands were going to drive a truck with all of our belongings from our house to the farm house. Brad took us to the car where Curtis was waiting and the drive from the airport to the farm seemed to take all day. It was way out in the middle of no where; I swear there was nothing around, we didn't even see anyone until we pulled up to the farm house. Brad showed me which bedroom was going to be mine and it was right across the hall from Curtis's room. My mom will stay in Brad's room all the way on the other side of the house. The house was very big and was so beautiful. That night I could hardly eat dinner or sleep, I had so much to do and I was so excited to see the whole farm and all the animals.

The next morning I woke up early and went downstairs to find my mom already in the kitchen cooking breakfast.

"Well hello sunshine." My mom said as she smiled at me.

"Good morning momma, why are you up so early?"

"Brad has to eat before he goes to work"

"But its Sunday! Why does he have to work?"

"He has to work on the farm and it's a 24 hour 7 days a week job"

"Well, when does he get to rest?"

"He finds time, thanks to all the farm hands he has helping him."

About that time a man came walking in the kitchen.

"Good morning family, my name is Josh and I am the foreman here."

"Good morning Josh I am Mary and this is my daughter Angela."

"It's very nice to meet you both! I'm sure you will be very happy here and if I can be of any service to you please just let me know!" He replied.

"Why thank you Josh, you're so very kind." My mom replied. "Angela, please go and set the table for breakfast."

"Okay momma. Are you going to eat with us, Mr. Josh?"

"Why yes I am, would you like me to help you with the table?"

"No thank you, I'll do it."

Brad and Curtis came downstairs and we all sat down at the table. Josh said grace and as he and Brad were fixing their plates they were talking about the farm. Josh ate very quickly, took a cup of coffee and left to get the other hands started.

Brad pushed his chair back and said; "Mary, school will start back next month and we need to get the kids ready for it. You need to take them into town for their yearly check up and get their school supplies. Winters can get pretty cold and rough around here so make sure you also get some proper clothing. Curtis and the ladies in the store will help you."

Brad then looked at me and said; "Education is very important and in this house I will not tolerate nothing less than a's and b's, do you understand me young lady?"

"Yes sir." I replied softly.

My mother responded by saying "Angela has always done very well in school."

"Good! We shouldn't have any problems then should we?" Brad said.

Nothing else was said as we ate our breakfast until mom got up and poured Brad a large cup of coffee. He stood up taking the coffee cup, kissing my mom on the cheek and said; "Mary you and the kids have a good day with your school shopping. Curtis you help them out and I'll see you all this evening." He gave my mom another kiss on the cheek and walked out the door.

Mom looked at us and said; "Alright children we have a lot to do today so we had better get started." Mom started cleaning up while Curtis and I finished eating. After the kitchen was cleaned we went into town, it was beautiful just like everything else here. The town was small and had that old look. It made you feel like you were in an old movie. We had to see the doctor first, he was old and funny. He told mom to just call him Doc and that his youngest son was going to take over his practice one day, but that would be years from now. He said that Curtis and I were in good health and he would like to give mom some advice to help us from getting sick a lot. He was afraid that my mom and I would get sick the most during our first year here, but we would get use to the weather soon enough.

Curtis and I played a lot together before school started back. He would take me fishing and he made me feel so special. I was the only one he would take to his favorite fishing hole. Curtis taught me how to fish, swim and ride a bike. One day I asked him "why are you so nice to me, after all we are going to be brother and sister soon and brothers are always mean to their sisters, not to mention I am younger than you?"

"It's not always like that." Curtis said laughingly. "Sometimes brothers and sisters do get along and become very close. Besides; you're the only friend I have; it's been pretty lonely here on the farm with no other kids around. The closest neighbor we have is over twenty miles from here."

A little confused I asked; "You don't have any friend's?"

"Yes, but their all from school and I don't get to see them during the summertime."

Before I could ask him another question he pushed me into the pond and then jumped in behind me.

We were having the best time but it was starting to get late. Curtis said; "Angela, we better start heading home for dinner."

As we were walking home I asked Curtis; "Do you remember anything about your mom?"

"No. When I was younger my dad showed me pictures of her and he would tell me stories, but I don't really remember anything. Sometimes I think I dream about her, but then I'm not really sure."

I felt a tear fall from my face when I asked him; "Do you miss her?"

"I guess I do, sometimes. But think about it, how do you miss someone or something you never really had in the first place? What about you Angela, do you miss your dad?"

"Yes, but he never really lived with us. I guess I was just use to him not being around much and when he was he didn't stay long. When he was around he would take me shopping or we would go to the park and have a picnic, things like that. But I don't really remember him spending time with momma or taking her anywhere like he did with me. Isn't that funny Curtis?"

"Yea, I guess so. Why didn't he stay at your house with you and your mom?"

"I really don't know! Once I asked him why he had to go and he just said; "Because it's time baby girl." I would ask my momma and she would just walk away, never saying a word."

"Well Angela; we're your family now and we won't leave you or your mom, I promise. We better hurry I'm sure dinner will be ready soon and if we don't get cleaned up before my dad gets home he won't be very happy."

"Okay" I said as we ran to the house and upstairs to our bedrooms.

My mom started calling for us; "Angela, Curtis. Hurry up dinners on the table and I don't want it to get cold."

When we got to the table we saw Brad laughing and saying; "So, how hungry are you two?" "Pretty hungry" Curtis said.

I laughed and said; "Yea, me too."

"Well have a seat and let's say grace before you fix your plates."

While Brad was saying grace I was thinking how happy we are going to be as a family. I wish we could have been a family with my real dad. But its okay, Curtis needed a mom. The only thing I didn't like so far was; we were not allowed to talk at the table unless we were spoken to. This was Brad's rule. My mom and I would use dinner time to talk about everything. I miss doing that with her. I miss doing a lot of things. Hopefully it will be better once the wedding is over.

When we finished dinner Brad told Curtis and me to clean up the table and the kitchen while they go up to their bedroom and finish with the wedding plans. "Plus it's been a long day and I have to get up early in the morning, there's no rest for me on this farm."

"Yes sir" Curtis said.

We cleaned off the table and took everything to the kitchen. Curtis got down the bowls and lids so we could put all the leftovers in containers and then place them in the refrigerator.

"Okay Angela." Curtis said; "You can use this step stool to stand on while you wash the dishes and I will dry them. Once we finish up we can go to my room and play a game."

Time went by pretty fast and before we knew it the first day of school was here. I was scared and a little excited at the same time. Josh the Foreman, came by to see us off to school. Curtis tugged at my shirt and said; "Come on Angela, we have to walk to the end of the driveway to catch the bus and she won't wait for us."

Once we got to school Curtis took me all around the place and he checked up on me all day. It felt pretty good to have him do that. School went by pretty fast and on our way home Curtis asked me when my birthday was, so I said "I was born on Halloween, why? When's your birthday?"

"It's today. I'm twelve now." He replied.

"Does my mom know?"

"I don't know" he said sadly. "But dad told me a long time ago he would give me a gun when I turned twelve, so I'm pretty excited about that."

When we got off the bus we both ran home as fast as we could. I was praying that they didn't forget with the wedding planning and all. Curtis opened the door to the house and it was so quite inside, no one was around. I could see Curtis's eyes begin to fill with water.

"Curtis, my mom was always home when I got off the bus before, where can she be?"

The back door opened and Brad walked in. "Come on you two and follow me, I need some help in the barn."

"Wait!" I yelled! I ran up to Brad and said; "Did you know today was Curtis's birthday?"

Brad looked at me with a very stern look and said; "I thought I just said come with me to the barn, I need you both to help me out!"

We didn't say another word as we walked into the barn. All of a sudden the music started playing and everyone started singing Happy Birthday to Curtis. All the farm hands were laughing and Josh was playing his guitar. Curtis started laughing and went around saying hello to everyone.

Josh and Curtis were very close, they grew up together. Josh had finished high school just a couple of years ago. He and his father both worked and lived on the farm. They moved on the farm when Josh was three, the farm was all Josh knew. His mom left them shortly after he was born and his dad passed away eight months ago. Brad told Josh he could stay on and asked him to take the foreman's job.

I grabbed Brad's hand and said; "I'm sorry I shouldn't have spoken that way to you."

He picked me up and said; "It's okay little one, its okay." He gave me the biggest hug ever and put me back down. Later we had cake and ice cream while we watched Curtis open his gifts. We were having such a wonderful time but, it was getting late and mom told us to get ready for bed. She reminded us that we had school the next day. I was so pumped from the party I could hardly go to sleep. Brad and mom walk into my room and gave me a hug and kiss good night. My mom use to do it all the time but not since we moved here. I finally felt like I was in a real family. I was going to have a full time dad, a real brother and everything is going to be alright.

School was going pretty good, but it was getting colder and it was a long walk to the end of the driveway. On some days I would whine and Curtis would grab my hand and practically drag me to the bus stop. Brad would get really angry if we missed the bus or if he saw me pouting. When no one was looking I would kick or hit Curtis for pulling me, but that never stopped him. I knew deep down he was only trying to protect me from getting a spanking, but it was getting so cold and I didn't like having to walk so far. I would beg mom to drive us to the end of the driveway and to let us sit in the car while we waited for the bus. Sometimes she would, but if Brad found out he would fuss at her and at us, then he would give us more chores to do that afternoon. I didn't understand what the big deal was, at times I felt like Brad was just being mean.

One morning the wind was blowing so hard it felt like it was cutting right through me and I started to cry. I begged mom to drive us but Brad said no. Curtis took my hand and as we were walking out the front door I cried out loud that I wanted to go back to my real home, at least there the bus would pick me up in front of my house. When we stepped off the porch Curtis told me to climb on his back and he would carry me to the bus stop. I don't know how he put up with me. Once we got to the bus stop he would sit down and put me in his lap. He held me as tight as he could and he would rock me back and fourth as if I were a baby. It wasn't long and I was warm and stopped crying. Curtis would baby me something awful and I liked it. My mom didn't do it very much anymore, she was too busy with other things and wasn't able to spend anytime with me. I was missing my real dad so much, I would have dreams that he was on his way to pick me up.

Time was going by so quickly and before I knew it, Halloween was here and so was my birthday. I can't wait to see what they are going to do for me. Curtis and I rushed home and ran to the barn but it was locked. My mom called out to us to come into the house. Once inside she told us to go upstairs and change. Curtis and I found Halloween costumes on our beds and Brad had invited all of our friends and a lot of his friends to the house. When we got back downstairs Brad yelled; "Hey little one."

"Yes sir." I cried, as I ran to him.

He picked me up and said; "We are going to have a Halloween party and your birthday party all in one, is that okay?"

"Yes sir," I said with excitement.

"Just look at you two in your costumes, you both look adorable." My mother said. "Come on everyone lets go the barn."

"But momma, Curtis and I ran to the barn when we got home, but it was locked."

"That's because we weren't ready for you to go in yet." She said as she laughed. Brad was laughing too as he opened the door.

I got a horse for my birthday. I was so excited that I wanted to ride him right then.

"Wait a minute little one." Brad said. "You can't ride him yet; you'll have to wait until we can teach you, other wise you could get hurt."

Curtis and Josh spoke up at the same time saying they would teach me how to ride him.

As the night went on some of Brad's friends would call me and tell me to come see them. When I asked why, they would say, just so they could talk to me and then they would sit me on their lap. It was getting a little scary because they would rub my legs or back and at times play with my hair and tell me how pretty I was. They would hug me very tightly and it would make me feel very uncomfortable. I told this to Curtis but not to anyone else. Curtis told me to be very careful with some of those men, they would do me harm. Curtis would catch those guys messing with me and he would come over and tell me that my mom wanted to see me right now. Curtis would take my hand and we would walk away. When we were out of site Curtis said: "Next time act like you don't hear them and turn the other way and walk off."

I kept looking for my real dad to show up, but he never did. I just don't understand he never misses my birthday. I asked my mom if she knew where he was but she said no. She said it was getting late so Curtis and I should get off to bed. Later that night Curtis came to my room and said; "Angela what's wrong? Why are you crying? Didn't you like your birthday party?"

"Yes." I told him. "It really was a lot of fun. I just thought my dad would be here, he never missed my birthday before."

"I'm sorry." Curtis said as he wrapped his arm around me. "I'm sure he was trying to get here, maybe something happened and he just couldn't make it. I'm sure he will be in touch really soon. Here I'll stay with you until you fall asleep."

CHAPTER TWO

The school year went by so fast. Curtis was a little upset because he wouldn't be able to see his friends for several months. I for one thought it was great. I couldn't wait to have Curtis all to myself again so we could go swimming and fishing. This summer was going to be the best. We had plans to ride our horses and were going camping.

As we were walking to the house and talking about our plans Curtis and I saw this new car in the driveway. Neither of us recognized it so we ran inside the house to find out who it was. In the living room I saw my real dad. He was sitting on the couch and my mom was sitting in her chair. Brad was sitting in his chair next to my mom and none of them looked very happy. I know my eyes must have looked like they were going to pop out of my head when I screamed out. "Daddy is that really you?" I screamed daddy again as I ran to him. "It's been so long, I miss you something awful. Do you know you missed my birthday? Why didn't you come?"

"I'm sorry sweetheart." He said as his grip tightened on me. "I tried but something came up and I just couldn't make it. It's a little hard for me now that you live so far away. But listen honey, I need to talk to you. I want you to come live with me for a while. I've remarried and you have been with your mother for so many years. I think it's time for you to move in with me now."

"No daddy, I don't want to leave momma. I have a real family now and I don't want to leave them either."

"I'm sorry baby girl but if you don't come with me now, I don't know when, or if, I will be back. Honey please you have to come with me now. We may never be able to see one another again."

I started crying as I pulled myself out of his arms. Then I became angry. "Don't you love me anymore daddy?"

"I love you more then anything else in this world and I'm so sorry, but that's just the way it is" "Why can't I spend time with you and Momma?"

"Baby, I have to leave and I need for you to give me an answer. Do you want to live with me?"

"I'm sorry daddy, I love you but I can't leave here, not right now."

My daddy got up and started walking towards the door. I could see tears in his eyes and yet he didn't say another word. My mom called me over to her. I watched my real daddy walk out the door. My heart felt like it was being torn from my chest and my throat felt like it was swelling. I pulled away from my mom and ran back towards my dad. I was crying out to him; "No daddy, please don't go I'm sorry. Daddy stop! Please don't leave me!"

He stopped, turned around and as he picked me up we both had tears falling down our faces like a waterfall. This was the first time I had seen my dad cry. I knew he needed me but so did my mom. What would Curtis do if I left? We have become so close and he needed me too. My dad kissed my cheek and said; "Hush my little one. Please don't cry anymore. I'll write to you often, and I promise that I will try my best to come see you when I can. Do you promise to write me back?"

"Yes daddy, I promise; and I'll send pictures so you won't forget what I look like."

"I could never forget your beautiful face, not ever. I love you with all my heart. I want you to know that I will always love you no matter where I am or who I'm with. I will always be there for you when ever you need me. If you ever decide you want to come live with me, I will be here faster then you can blink an eye. All you have to do is let me know when and where, I promise you that I will be there. Now give me a really big hug and kiss so I can go." My dad whispered in my ear; "Bye my baby girl. I love you and don't you ever forget that."

Still crying he slowly put me down and walked out the door. I didn't want him to leave but I couldn't go with him either. As I watched my dad walk out that door I fell to my knees. Even though my heart was screaming for him to come back, I didn't say it out loud. Brad picked me up and carried me to his big rocker recliner chair. He sat down placing me on his lap. He held me close to his chest and as he began rocking me he tightened his hold as if to make sure I wouldn't fall. I was crying so hard that I must have fallen to sleep.

When I woke up I was in my bed with Curtis lying beside me. He surprised me so I asked him; "What are you doing?"

"I didn't want you to wake up alone." Curtis said. "Don't you remember what I told you? I told you I would never leave you?"

"Yes you did, thank you."

As I pulled myself closer into his arms we laid there for a bit longer. Then I asked him; "Do you know if momma and Brad are awake yet?"

"They've been up for a couple of hours now and they're downstairs. I was told once you woke up I was to bring you down for breakfast."

"What! Did I sleep that long?"

"No you cried that long. Dad held you in his arms until 11:30 last night. He carried you up here and your mom put you into your pajamas. I asked her if I could stay with you just in case you woke up and she said yes. So, are you ready to eat? I'm about to starve. We didn't get to eat any dinner last night."

"You mean you haven't eaten since lunch yesterday?"

"That's right, so if you're ready so am I."

"Okay Curtis, let me get dressed and I'll be right down."

"Good, I'll tell them you're on your way."

While I was changing my clothes I started thinking about last night. I couldn't believe my dad just left me like that, and why couldn't he come back to see me? I just don't understand any of it. I slowly walked downstairs and into the kitchen. My mom was watching me as if she wasn't sure what to say. I looked at Brad and he said with a smile; "Good morning sunshine. I sure could use a really big hug this morning."

I smiled back at him as I walked over and put my arms around his neck. I squeezed him as hard as I could.

"Thanks for that big bear hug, boy I really needed that this morning. Now let me look at you, oh my goodness will you just look at that face. It's all swollen and red."

"Is it really?" I replied in horror.

"Well I'm only the foreman here, but I would have to say, yes." Josh said. "You know it looks like you were thrown into a bee hive and the bee's won."

"No it doesn't. Angela don't you listen to him" Curtis replied as he laughed.

Brad picked me up and put me on his lap. "Sunshine you're beautiful just like your mom."

Mom sat down at the table and Brad said; "Kids we have something to tell you."

"What's up dad?" Curtis asked.

As Brad smiled he said; "Mary and I have decided to get married this summer."

"In three weeks as a matter of fact." My mom responded.

It got so quite you could hear a pin drop. Brad put me down and as I sat in my chair at the table Brad said; "I want us to be a family. Angela I can't take the place of your dad, nor do I want to try, but I would like to be a dad to you!"

My mom looked at Curtis and said; "And I wouldn't dare try to replace your mom, but if it's okay with you Curtis, I would like to be a mother figure in your life. Your mom's memory will always be here and I wouldn't want it any other way."

Curtis wiped a tear from his eye as he said; "Yea, it would be nice to have a mom."

"Brad." I said. "I would like to have you as a dad."

"Great." Brad said. "I was hoping you kids would be happy about all that. Well then we have a lot to do between now and then. Curtis I will need your help and Angela I'm sure your mom will need you to help her as well. It's going to be the biggest thing that ever hit this farm or this town."

We all laughed and talked about what needed to be done as we ate our breakfast. I can't remember the last time I saw my mom laugh so much.

CHAPTER THREE

Brad was right; there was a lot to do before the wedding. Mom and Brad were married on the farm and it was beautiful. It was held outside with lights strung out everywhere. They had an all night party in the barn. Brad had a real band with singing and dancing and I have never seen so much food! The cake stood four layers high and Josh made ice-cream to go with it. I don't know who's getting the better end of the deal, Curtis getting a mom or me getting a full time dad.

Brad was taking mom to Florida for a four week honeymoon. Before leaving, Brad introduced me to a lady by the name of Ms. Amy and a man named Mr. Moore, whom Curtis already knew. Brad said Ms. Amy, Mr. Moore and Josh were going to watch over us while they were away and we were to mind our manners. Mom gave Curtis and me a kiss and hug goodbye and said she would miss us very much. Everyone threw bird seed at them as they ran to the car. Mom got us birdseed to throw because she didn't believe in wasting food. She said at least the birds could eat the seed.

Mr. Moore was at our house a lot while mom and Brad were away. Mr. Moore owns the farm next door to Brad's; I think he's really here to see Ms. Amy. He looked so young and he was very handsome. He and Josh almost looked like they could be brothers. They both had dark blue eyes, Mr. Moore had dark brown hair and Josh had light brown hair. Both had skin that was deeply tanned from the sun. As far as that goes, so did everyone else living around here that owned farms.

Every morning I would see Mr. Moore sitting at the breakfast table. He would ask me to sit by him and he would tell me stories of his up bringing and heritage. Mr. Moore was an Indian and said he didn't have any family left living. I liked Mr. Moore, he was funny and he said he liked spending time with me. Josh didn't seem to like him much and he didn't like him hanging around me. I asked Curtis about Mr. Moore and he said he was okay and he was good friends with his dad, but other then that he didn't know too much more about him.

One morning after breakfast, Mr. Moore and I went horse back riding. We rode over to his house. I swear, every time I go to someone's house around here theirs is bigger then the one before. His house was the biggest by far. There were flowers and bushes that wrapped around the porch and his grass was the greenest I have ever seen! Mr. Moore invited me in to get something cold to drink. "Angela." He said. "Will you please call me Daniel? After all we are friends aren't we?"

"Why yes I guess so." I replied.

As we sat on the porch drinking our sodas we were talking all about my mom and my real dad. But I wanted to hear more about him being an Indian. So I asked; "If you're Indian then how come your name doesn't sound like it?"

Daniel laughed and said; "My father was half white from his father's side. The rest of my family and blood line is Indian."

"Oh, I guess that would explain it." I then couldn't resist saying; "Daniel do you know you and Josh look alike? I bet you could pass as brothers."

"Yes." He said. "You know there is a story behind that and maybe one day I will tell you about it. How about us going to the kitchen and I will fix us some lunch and after we eat we'll ride back to your place?"

"That sounds good to me." I said.

I was having a wonderful time with Daniel, that is, until I got home and Josh started yelling at me. "What do you think you are doing?

Confused by his question I asked; "What do you mean?"

"What has Mr. Moore been saying to you? What have you two been doing?" Josh screamed.

"He's been telling me about his family and I really don't think it's any of your business?" I screamed back.

"Well Ms. Smarty britches, you don't need to spend so much time alone with that man!"

"Why, I don't understand? He's been very nice to me and he's my friend."

Josh looked at me with very angry eyes and said, "Angela I am forbidding you to talk to him anymore!"

"You're not my father and he's looking after us too!" I replied back very angrily.

Curtis walked into the house and Josh responded to him by saying; "Curtis you better talk to your sister. She's spending a lot of time alone with Mr. Moore and she's even calling him by his first name and you know your dad will have a fit about that."

"He's right Angela. You better not let dad hear you call Mr. Moore by his first name and you really shouldn't be spending so much time with him alone."

"You're not the boss of me Curtis."

Josh slumped over and said; "Please Angela, I know what I'm talking about."

"Okay fine. I don't understand, but I won't go off with him anymore. But can either of you tell me what the big deal is?"

Josh looked at me with the saddest look and said; "One day you'll find out, but for right now thank you for trusting us on this."

The next morning everyone was working on the house to welcome Mom and Brad home. We are expecting them back this evening. The phone rang and Ms. Amy answered it. She looked a little sad as she called out to us. "Curtis, Angela that was your parents. They said they were very sorry but they weren't going to make it home tonight. They said not to worry because they will be here as soon as they can tomorrow."

Curtis and I were so disappointed; we were looking forward to seeing them. We had worked all day putting up welcome back posters that we had made the night before. Ms. Amy and I made a really nice dinner and Mr. Moore let me pick some of his flowers to set on the table. Josh put up one of the welcome back banners we made on the front porch.

"So what do we do now?" I asked Ms. Amy.

"Oh, come on now." She said. "Stop with all the ugly faces and let's enjoy our dinner, if you hurry off to bed morning will be here before you know it."

Ms. Amy had beautiful long black hair with light hazel green eyes. When she looked at you she made you feel like you should bow or something. She was so kind to Curtis and me. We did just as she said, we ate, we cleaned up and we went right to bed.

The next morning when I woke up I ran downstairs to see if I could help Ms. Amy with breakfast just in case my mom and Brad where to come home this morning. Only when I got to the kitchen it was my mom standing at the stove, I almost fell to the floor from the shock.

"Momma, is that you?" I said softly.

She turned around and laughingly said; "Yes it's me my little sunshine?"

"Oh momma I've missed you so much." I cried as I ran into her arms almost knocking her over. "Easy there my little one, did you miss me that much?"

"Yes I did, I don't ever want you to go away again."

"Oh, my beautiful little girl, I promise I will never leave you again. Now will you be a good little girl and set the table for me, your father will be down shortly?"

"Okay." I said and as she was handing me the plates I asked her; "Do I have to call him daddy?"

"It would be very nice if you did after all Curtis is going to call me mom. You know Angela it would make it feel like we were a real family. Don't you think so?"

"Yes, I guess so."

"Honey, Brad doesn't want to take the place of your dad; no body could ever do that. He just wants to be a part of your life and be a daddy figure. Don't you want that too?"

"I see what your saying momma and yea I do."

"That's my girl, now go set the table for breakfast."

Curtis and Brad came down the stairs right as we were putting the last of the food on the table. Brad looked at me and said; "Good morning and how are my two favorite girls?"

I giggled and said; "Good morning daddy."

He looked at me with a strange look on his face and said; "Angela, will you come here to me please."

For a minute I thought I had done something wrong. Slowly I walked over to Brad and he picked me up and said; "My cute little darling."

He hugged me tightly and placed me in my chair. Curtis laughed and said; "Good morning Angela and good morning to you too mom."

My mom smiled and told him good morning back. We all started laughing and talked about what had gone on for the past four weeks.

Once breakfast was over dad had to meet up with Josh to see what was going on with the farm and Curtis went with him. Mom and I cleaned up the dishes and picked up around the house. We walked down to the garden to pick some vegetables so we could do some canning for the winter. The day went by so fast and before we knew it we had to get cleaned up for dinner. Dinner went by quickly and not much talking took place. I guess everyone was tired.

"Curtis, Angela, will you two please take care of the dishes and kitchen, your mother and I have an early day tomorrow."

"Yes sir." Curtis and I both replied as they kissed us good night.

"Curtis." I said. "They didn't say much tonight and they were in a hurry to go to bed. Do you know why?"

Curtis just laughed at me. "What's so funny? My mom and I would always watch a movie before we went to bed and momma hasn't done that with me since we got here."

"I'm sorry Angela." Curtis said. "But I don't think your mom is thinking of that right now."

"WHY?" I said angrily!

"Because they do other things together and we can't be a part of it."

I started crying as I washed the dishes. "Curtis I don't think my mom loves me as much as she use to now that she has your dad?"

28

"Oh no Angela, it's not like that at all. They have to spend time alone for a while and then they will spend time with us again, you'll see."

"I don't understand any of this, how do you know what will happen? They've been alone for four weeks already, how much more time do they need?"

Curtis put his arm around me and said; "Please don't cry Angela, I'll watch a movie with you and I'll even fix us some popcorn, Okay?"

"Really; you'll do that for me?" I said as I sniffled and tried to hold back more tears.

Curtis wiped my eyes with his towel and said, "Yes Angela I will. After all you are my sister now and I don't want to see you hurting, so please will you stop crying?"

"Okay. Curtis. I love you."

"I love you too, now if you don't hurry up we won't have time to watch a movie."

We hurried to finish up so we could go into the living room. Curtis told me to pick out any movie I wanted to watch while he made the popcorn. We curled up on the couch with blankets, ate popcorn and watched our movie. I was getting sleepy and Curtis told me if I fell asleep he would carry me upstairs when the movie was over.

The next morning I woke up in my bed. My first thought was; boy this seams to be happening to me a lot lately. As I walked downstairs to get something to drink my mom was already up. She was in the kitchen cooking breakfast. "Momma how come we don't watch movies or talk anymore?" I asked her.

"Oh honey I am so sorry. We will again real soon I promise, just right now I like spending time with your new daddy."

It wasn't long after that when we started spending time together again and Curtis was spending time with his dad. I was so excited when I received a letter from my real dad today. We started writing to each other just about every week. Then it was about once a month. All of a sudden his letters just stopped coming. I wrote several more times but never received another letter back. I just didn't understand it. This was the only contact we had and I never saw him again either. Sometimes at night I would pull out the letters he had sent me and I would read them all over again. I would pretend it was a new letter then I would cry myself to sleep. In the last letter I received from him he told me about the twins he and Melody had. I never got to meet her but they have a daughter named Glenda and a son named Alex. I guess I will never get to meet them either. I wonder if my dad ever told them about me. I guess he no longer needs me since he has another daughter, one that didn't refuse to live with him. I asked mom if she knew why he doesn't write me anymore and she said; "Angela honey, you both have families now. Maybe he felt you both would be happier just to be with the families you have."

"Do you think he still loves me?"

"Do you still love him?"

"Yes I do, very much."

"Well, I know he still loves you too. I'm sure his love is so strong for you that he decided to let you live a normal life with the family you have now. I think you should give him the same respect."

Mom wiped the tears from my eyes and told me not to cry about it anymore. She said I have her, Brad, Curtis and Josh now. I should be happy to have such a loving family. I guess she's right, but that doesn't make me miss my daddy any less.

CHAPTER FOUR

The years went by very quickly here on the farm. I'm now thirteen and Curtis is seventeen. Curtis is graduating this year. We've become very close. He's talked to me a lot about what he wants to do with his life and it doesn't include the farm. He wants to go into the military and one day he hopes to own a business in town. I don't want him to leave. He's my brother and I love him, sometimes I think I love him more than just a brother, but I don't dare speak of it. He made me promise to keep his secret of wanting to go into the military. He didn't want anyone else to know, especially dad. Curtis knew dad wouldn't approve of it and with mom getting sick so much, Curtis didn't want to worry her.

Mom stays in bed more and more everyday. We noticed the doctor was coming out to the house a lot to see her. Every winter she would get sick and every year the sickness got worse. We over heard the doctor telling dad he didn't know what more he could do for her but he did know of a doctor that has dealt with her illness before and that he would give him a call. I wasn't sure what he meant but I could see by the look on Curtis's face mom had more than a cold or flu.

Dad wasn't as happy as he used to be and we didn't see him very much either. He was always busy and it seemed like he always had something to do or somewhere to go. Sometimes it felt like he was just avoiding spending time with us altogether. Dad use to have a drink once in awhile on the weekend but now, I am really getting worried about him. His drinking is getting out of control. I've spoken to Cutis and Josh about it, but they don't know what's going on with him either. He's now drinking during the week and very heavy on the weekends.

Sometimes late at night, dad would lie down beside me and tell me about his day as he held me in his arms. I wouldn't say a word, I would just listen to him talk. Him and mom would sit and talk for hours about what went on during the day and I knew he was missing that. Sometimes he would lie beside me and not say anything. When daylight would break he would kiss me on the cheek or forehead, get up and say he needed to change clothes. Then he would look back at me and say; "Honey will you please go fix me some breakfast?" And of course I would. On those nights I could see him wipe the tears from his eyes almost the entire night and he would try his best not to let me see him. I wish there was something I could do for the both of them, but what?

It was taking its toll on Curtis too. I would catch him sit at mom's bedside reading her a book and when he would walk out of the room, I could see the redness in his eyes. I had to take on the responsibility of watching over him and dad. The nights would last forever; there were times I could hardly keep my eyes open at school from being so tired. I don't know what daddy would do if he didn't have all the farm hands to help him out. My heart went out to Josh as well, I've seen times when his hands would bleed. When he showed up for dinner I would try my best to wrap them up and tell him he was working his hands literally to the bone. I even caught him falling asleep at the table while he was trying to eat. There were several nights he didn't come to the house for dinner so I would fix a plate and take it to him. He was staying in the cabin by the lake on the other side of the farm. I would have to talk non stop to him so I could keep him awake just long enough to eat something. During this time we had got to know each other and we became very close.

One night Josh kissed me on the forehead just like he had done so many times before, but this time his kiss felt different and then he kissed me on the cheek. He looked into my eyes and I into his as he bent over and kissed me on the lips. I can't explain it but for some reason, this kiss was very different, it was giving me an uneasy feeling inside. Josh took me into his arms and kissed me again only this time it was a bit firmer. He placed his hand inside my shirt and squeezed my breast. I became scared and tried to pull myself away from him only to have him tighten his grip on me. He moved his hand from my breast and placed it on the inner part of my thigh. Once again I tried to push him away. His hand then started going up my dress and inside my underwear. I knew I had to stop him, so I bit his lip and blood started shooting out. He screamed and pulled away which gave me the time to get up and run. I could hear him calling out to me telling me how sorry he was, but I just kept running. Several months went by and we never said a word about it.

Coming home from school one day Curtis and I saw dad standing on the porch. We could see by the look on his face something was wrong. He told us that mom wasn't feeling well and he would need us to pick up more of the work load. He told Curtis: "Son I'll need your help around the yard and farm."

Sure dad, no problem." Curtis replied quickly.

Daddy then looked at me and said; "Angela you will have to take over all the cooking and cleaning. Ms. Amy has agreed to help you out until you can handle it on your own."

"Okay daddy, can I see momma now?"

"After while honey, she's sleeping right now. Ms. Amy is inside to teach you a few things, so will you go on into the kitchen."

"Yes daddy." I said. I really wanted to see momma, but I wasn't about to make a fuss. So I went to the kitchen and told Ms. Amy hello.

"Why hello there little one and how are you today?" She said.

"I'm good I guess. Do you know what's going on with my mom?"

"Not a whole lot, except they put your mom on a feeding tube today. The doctor will be by later tonight to show us what to do. Your dad's been pretty evasive about everything else. Look I know it's going to be hard around here for a little while, but I want you to know that I'm here to help. I plan on staying here during the week and then I'm afraid you will be on your own on the weekend. There's so much I can still teach you on cooking, cleaning and sewing. Honey look anytime you need someone to talk to you I'm here."

"Thank you. I just wish I knew what's going on with my mom; and

Ms. Amy, I'm not trying to be rude or anything, but you know I've helped my mom cook and I've been doing most of the cooking and cleaning for some time here on my own."

"Yes I do know that, but there is so much more you can still learn. Things you will need to know if you're going to run this farm one day plus, I know so many short cuts that will help you out on the days you are over loaded."

"What are you talking about, why would I want to run this farm?"

"That will be your job as the lady of the house."

"My mom is the lady of the house not me."

"I know but, one day you will be. Sweetie please stop questioning me and let's get started or do I have to call your father in here?"

"No Ms. Amy, I'm sorry. It's very kind of you to help us out and it was wrong of me to question you like that."

"It's alright child, now lets get started before your father gets back and finds he has no hot meal on the table."

I know Ms. Amy means well and she is a very kind and gentle person. I know I can learn a lot more from her. I just don't like the way she says things sometimes. I didn't understand why she never married either. Maybe she and Mr. Moore will marry one day. The doctor did come back. He, Ms. Amy and I went to mom's room. He showed us everything we would need to do and what to watch for. Doc told me I would need to help bathe her and as time goes by I would have to do more to help out. I tried to get some information out of the doctor about my mom's condition, only he said I would have to talk to my dad.

CHAPTER FIVE

For the past few years Ms. Amy has been here to meet me after school. With us spending so much time together, we've became close. She was like a second mother to me and she did teach me a lot just like she said she could. Everyone said they couldn't tell the difference between my cooking and hers anymore. I've become a wiz at sewing too; I made new curtains for the kitchen. I've canned fruits and vegetables and I learned how to make jelly and syrup. We have the pantry so completely stocked that it could last for several winters to come. Ms. Amy has bee hives on her property and she even taught me how to preserve the honey. She gave me the jars I made to put in our panty. It's been quite a lot of work doing all this and keeping up my school work, but in an odd way it's also been fun.

Mr. Moore would help me with school work when Curtis was busy with dad. Josh would help me from time to time when ever he could. He told me one night how proud he was of me and how I was growing up to be a very beautiful lady. We finally talked about what had happened that night between us so long ago. We admitted to each other there did seem to be some feelings between us. Sometimes I would go to his cabin and we would talk for hours. We both felt good about getting some of that day to day stuff off our chest. I'm not going to lie, we did have some heated moments between us, but when I pushed him or told him no he would stop. I told him how I would spend as much time as I could with mom but most of the time, she didn't even know I was in the room with her. Curtis would read to her every night and I didn't have the heart to tell him that she didn't know who he was or even that he was in the room half the time. She did have some good moments once in awhile, when that happened she would talk as if she had been having regular conversations with us all the long. It was during those moments; we were all talking so fast to her in fear she would slipped away again.

Doc was coming to the house to see mom regularly now. I have this feeling she's not going to pull out of her illness this time. I'll never forget that one evening when doc came by to see mom. I was cooking dinner when he came downstairs and he didn't look too happy. He asked me to find my father. He needed to see him right away.

"Why I asked? Is mom okay?"

I could tell by the look in his eyes he was worried as he quietly responded; "Please get your father Angela."

I ran out the back door and right into one of the farm hands.

"Please find my dad, tell him Doc needs to see him right away, and hurry."

It only took a few minutes before Dad, Josh and Curtis all ran into the house.

I told dad; "Doc went back upstairs to mom's room."

Dad ran up the stairs. A couple of hours went by before they came down again. Curtis, Josh and I were sitting on the bottom step waiting for them to tell us something. Doc walked to the front door and stopped, never saying a word to anyone. Dad looked at us and you could tell he had been crying. With his voice cracking Brad said; "Angela, will you please get dinner on the table? Boys I need for you to get the hay in the barn before it gets any darker."

We didn't ask any questions. I walked into the kitchen and the boys went on outside. I went to the kitchen doorway where I could see both doc and dad standing at the front door. Dad had open the door for Doc and I heard him ask; "What's happening doc? What's going on with Mary?" "I'm sorry Brad, things aren't getting any better and time is running out for her. I'm afraid all we can do now, is keep her on pain killers so she doesn't have to go through any suffering. You can only do so much, but when the cancer spreads it's only a matter of time. I'll need to get the proper equipment so we can have her on a constant drip of medication. Brad I have to tell you, this is also going to be very costly."

"Doc, I've been finding the money this far and I will continue, so you get what ever it is that she needs."

"Alright Brad, I'll get everything set up as soon as I can. I'm also going to have a nurse come by daily to check on her. Everyone already knows how to work the feeding tube, but with everything else she's going to be connected to will have to be monitored very closely. I'll have the nurse show Angela and Ms. Amy what to do and what to watch for as well. My other advice is to you my friend; please tell your kids everything before it's too late."

"Now doc, you leave that to me, I'll tell them when the time is right."

The doctor left and I ran to daddy and asked; "Daddy what's going on with mom?"

He turned his head away from me and said; "Not to worry little one, everything will be just fine. Did you get dinner on the table?"

"No sir, but I'll do right now."

No one spoke during dinner and Josh didn't show up at all. When dad and Curtis finished eating, dad said he was going to lie down. Curtis said he was going to take a shower. I cleaned the kitchen and took a plate of food to Josh. I knocked and Josh didn't open his door nor did he answer me when I called out his name.

"Josh open up it's me Angela and I have your dinner."

Still Josh didn't open the door, so I placed the tray of food on the porch rail and opened the door myself. I grabbed the plate and went inside.

"It's a fine thing when a girl brings food to a hungry man and he doesn't even open the door for her. Josh where are you?"

I placed the food on the table. This wasn't like him not to answer me when I called out for him. I was getting worried so I started looking around the house when I noticed a light shining behind the cabin. I walk outside to see what it was and from the distance it looked like Josh swimming in the pond. As I walked towards him I began calling out his name and noticed a towel hanging over a tree branch.

"What are you doing? Can't you see I'm in the pond?" Josh cried out.

"Why yes I can dear sir and would this be your towel?" I said as I laughed pulling the towel from the branch.

"Yes, now put it back down!"

I took the towel laughing as I began running up towards the cabin. I could hear Josh getting out of the water calling out my name.

"Angela if you know what's good for you, you better drop that towel or you're going to be sorry."

I was losing my breath from laughing so hard. I haven't laughed like that in such a very long time. Half way up to the cabin I felt Josh grab me from behind and he knocked me down to the ground and fell on top of me, it took my breath away.

"Angela, Angela, please talk to me, are you okay?"

I started laughing so hard I lost my breath again and he started laughing at me laughing until we both just couldn't stop. But when we did stop and I looked up at Josh and he looked down at me it was like there was nothing else around. Josh kissed me right on the lips. My whole body went limp and I found myself kissing him back. My heart started pounding like it was going to pound right out of my chest. Josh slightly rose up; we became lost in each others eyes. We have all had so much on our minds lately and we were all getting so tired. For a brief moment in each others arms, it was like the world was so far behind us. I then started coming to my senses and realized that Josh was still on top of me and it felt like a stick was pushing against my thigh. Oh no, it hit me that Josh had no clothes on. I didn't move I couldn't even make a sound. All I could do was look at him and we started kissing again. I could feel his hands going up my shirt and touching my bare skin. I had chill bumps all over my body. Josh's body was cold at first but now he was starting to feel warm. As my senses went back out the window, Josh started unzipping my pants and pulling them downward. My body began to shiver, but I did nothing to stop him. He looked at me as if to see what I was going to do. I still did nothing. His lips moved to my neck and my whole body felt like it was on fire even though I was shivering. I felt Josh's fingers stroking me and the moisture began running down. Josh was beginning to position himself and I knew what was about to happen and yet I couldn't make myself stop him. My heart was saying this is wrong, my head was telling my body to move, yet I still did nothing. I heard my name being called. Oh my heaven it was Curtis! I panicked and pushed Josh off me and pulled myself up as I pulled my clothes back over me. What was I thinking?

As I started running to the house I never looked back. It was dark and I ran right into Curtis.

"Where were you?" He said.

Almost out of breath I replied. "I just took Josh his dinner."

"Oh, then why are you so wet and why is your face so red?"

"It's none of your business, now let go of me."

I jerked away from Curtis and took off towards the house again when I heard Josh calling for me. Curtis grabbed my hand and pulled me until I stopped walking.

"Now do you want to tell me what just took place between you and Josh or do I need to have a talk with Josh myself."

"No! Just let it go. It's none of your business. I'm not a little girl anymore so get use to it."

"What was going on between you and Josh?" Curtis said in a very strong tone.

"Curtis, what makes you think you were going to walk in on something?"

"I think you better get home, I'm going down to see Josh and I will be up in a minute."

Curtis turned me loose and started back down to the pond. I ran and grabbed his arm and begged him not to go and I told him I would explain everything. Curtis turned around and put his arm around me as we both walked back up to the house. We walked home slowly while I told him just enough to calm him down and no more. I guess it worked because he didn't go back to talk to Josh.

We found dad passed out in his chair from drinking and decided to leave him there. While I was lying in my bed I was thinking of Josh and I began to giggle. It was pretty funny and I couldn't stop thinking about the fact I saw him naked. He did have a pretty hot body; I never noticed all the muscles he had before and he was definitely well built in all aspects. My mind started to wander off when I heard my door slowly open.

"Can I come in?" Curtis asked.

"You know you can." I replied.

For the first time I noticed my brother's body as well. He was so vary tanned and he too had a very handsome build. He had deep dark blue eyes and shoulder length dirty blonde hair that was somewhat wavy. His eye lashes were long and dark and he had a very strong looking face. Oh my goodness, what am I doing? I can't be looking at my brother in this way. I should be ashamed of myself, what has Josh done to me!

"Angela, we need to talk." Curtis said.

"Okay, what about?"

"About what happened tonight between you and Josh?"

"Curtis I would rather not talk about it if you don't mind."

"Angela, I think we need to if it's what I think it was, and if I'm right, it could have turned into something you might not be ready for."

"Will you stop it, you're just over reacting!"

"Angela, you're a very beautiful girl and you're body is developing quite nicely, and guys are going to notice you more and more everyday."

"What are you saying Curtis? Have you noticed the changes taking place?"

"To be perfectly honest with you, yes I have."

"Oh! Well what do you see?"

"I see a very pretty girl that is growing into a beautiful young lady."

"If you weren't my brother would you want me?"

"Angela, I don't think you need to talk that way."

"Why are you scared to answer the question?"

"Okay yes, I would and just for the record we are only brother and sister by marriage, there is a difference you know."

We both stared at each other without saying another word. Curtis smiled and turned away to walk back out the door.

"Curtis, if we weren't related by marriage would you like me in a girlfriend way?"

"Angela we really don't need to go there, now stop thinking like that."

"Why? It's only a question?"

Curtis walked over to the bed and as he looked into my eyes he placed his hand behind my head. He laid me down to the pillow and was pulling the covers over me at the same time. He bent over and softly kissed me. It felt like we both had just melted into one as his simple kiss turned into both of us kissing. I could feel the pressure of his lips on mine and the heat between us as Curtis was slowly climbing into my bed. We heard our dad coming up the stairs and Curtis jumped up and ran out my room. I couldn't sleep after that, all I could think of was the kiss I received from two guys and how each one made me feel. I must be losing my mind to have so many thoughts going at me all at once.

When morning came, Curtis and Josh both kept their distance from me. I began thinking that I had done something wrong to make them avoid me this way. They both ate breakfast and left without saying a word.

Dad laughed and said; "Well little one, I guess they're in a hurry to get to work and I better do the same. Love you and I will see you at lunch time."

Daddy was the only one who showed up for lunch and at dinner it was so very quiet. Josh and Curtis didn't say a word and wouldn't even look at me. Josh left right after he finished eating and Curtis went right to bed. Dad headed out the door and said he was going out for a while. Once I finished cleaning up, I sat out on the porch looking at the stars and wondering what had happened. As the night went on I couldn't stop thinking how neither one of them would look at me or talk to me. I finally went inside locking up for the night. I checked in on mom and decided I needed to talk to Curtis to find out what is going on. Only I found that Curtis had locked his door. I was so confused to why his door was locked; we never locked our doors before. Why won't he talk to me?

41

Days went by with Josh and Curtis both ignoring me and it was ripping me up inside. Even thought mom wasn't awake to talk to me I would talk to her about Josh but not Curtis. One evening dad said he needed to go into town and he would have to stay the night. Once he left I locked up as I do every night. Only tonight, while I was lying in my bed I decided I was going to make Curtis talk to me but his door was locked again. Tears came to my eyes at the thought I had done something so awful to Curtis that he would lock me out. I turned around to go back to my room when I heard his door unlock. I walked back turned the knob again and the door opened, but his room was so dark, darker then normal.

"Curtis, Curtis where are you, it's so dark in here I can't see a thing. Why don't you have your small light on or your curtains open?"

"I'm here in the bed Angela, what do you want?"

I closed the door and slowly I tried to find my way to his bed. I felt Curtis take my hand and pull me down beside him. Before I could say a word he began kissing me as he pulled the covers over us. He then started pulling my gown up and started putting his hands on my breast. I knew I needed to stop him but I couldn't, or maybe I didn't want to.

"Curtis, what are you doing? I don't think we should be doing this, what if dad and mom were to find out?"

Curtis stopped and started pushing me out of his bed.

"Curtis what are you doing?"

"You have to go now, you can't stay here and I can't go to your room anymore either."

"I don't understand Curtis, what did I do?"

"You didn't do anything wrong, I'm the one in the wrong. Even though were not related by blood, we are by marriage and I refuse to do anything that would disgrace or defame you in anyway."

"Curtis what's happening to us?"

"Angela don't you get it; I'm in love with you. I have loved you from the first day I saw you. And not just in a sister and brother way either. I have loved you for a long time, and I will continue to love you no

42

matter what, but if you stay in here with me or I go to your room something will happen between us because I won't be able to stop myself. Now please go back to your room."

"But, Curtis.

"Please Angela will you just go."

As I walked out and went back to my room my heart felt so heavy and broken. I think I understand how Curtis feels about me because I have always felt that way about him. I knew when we were children that I loved him and not just as a brother. I also know if our parents were not married Curtis and I would have been able to pursue our feelings for each other. That night I cried myself to sleep knowing Curtis would stay away from me. We'll never lie next to each other again. I'll never feel the comfort or security from his arms anymore. I knew things would be different between us and I guess over time I'll be able to accept it. It's tearing me up inside knowing I will never be with the one man I truly love.

CHAPTER SIX

After Curtis's graduation he finally told dad he wanted to go into the military and start his own business in town when he gets out. Only dad went crazy and told him there was no way in hell he could do that to him. Dad told Curtis he needed him to stay and help run the farm. Curtis was so upset and told him he had plenty of farm hands and he had Josh. He was only being selfish by trying to make him stay.

"I'm sorry Curtis." Dad said; "I should have told you both the truth a long time ago. I can't afford to keep the workers on the farm any longer. They did agree to stay until the end of next month. I will only have Josh, you and your sister to help me after that."

'Dad what happened? Why can't they stay?" I asked him.

"Because I can't afford to pay them anymore, I've spent everything I had for Mary's doctors and medical supplies."

Curtis dropped his head and said; "I didn't know things had gotten that bad. I'll stay and help for now, but you do understand that one day I will have to leave."

"Thank you son and I do understand. I want you to be able to live your life and go after your dreams. I want your sister to be able to do the same thing."

Dad reached out and gave Curtis a hug and a pat on the back. "You do know I love you kids very much."

"I know dad and we love you too. Don't worry about a thing I'll stay as long as I can."

I was so proud of both of them for being so understanding of each other.

Josh and I started talking again and there were times I would catch him watching me. I could also tell it was getting harder for Curtis to keep his distance. When ever Josh would talk to me I could see Curtis watching us. Sometimes he would interrupt us by telling me dad needed me to do something. I think Josh was starting to notice Curtis's reaction towards us, because whenever he would ask me to go swimming or if he wanted to talk to me he would do it when Curtis wasn't around. There were times when Josh and I were alone that I could tell he wanted to kiss me. Some times he would get a little forceful but I was always able to get him to stop.

Ms. Amy is still coming over from time to time to help us out. Mostly during the day while I'm at school. One night she stayed after dinner to talk to dad. Mr. Moore showed up and said he needed to talk to Brad in private. Ms. Amy came into the kitchen where I was and told me she heard Mr. Moore tell my dad he had a business proposal for him as they walked out onto the front porch. I'm not sure what it was all about, but my dad became so angry at Mr. Moore that he told him to get off his property and told him to never step another foot over here again. Ms. Amy told me and Curtis to go upstairs and get ready for bed. Later that night dad came to our rooms and told us that doc would be here very early in the morning to check on mom so we better get some sleep. I heard him walk back down the stairs where he and Ms. Amy were talking. I stood at the top of the stairs to see if I could hear what they were talking about but then they walked outside.

"Angela." Curtis yelled. "Go to bed right now!"

"Okay fine." I said as I walked into my room.

Daddy didn't come lay with me that night and I was worried about him. I went looking for him but I couldn't find him anywhere so I went to talk to Curtis. Surprisingly he didn't have the door locked this time so I walked right in. I closed the door behind me and started walking over to his bed when I hit my toe on the leg of his bed.

"What are you doing in here?" Curtis said quietly.

"I'm sorry Curtis, but I needed to talk to you about dad, I'm worried."

Curtis reached out for my hand to help guide me towards him.

"Why do you keep it so dark in here?" I asked.

"So little girls like you can't find their way."

"You don't have to be so rude. I'm worried about dad but never mind, I'll talk to Josh tomorrow."

I went to head back towards the door when Curtis jumped up and put his arms around me.

"I'm so sorry, I didn't mean to snap at you but you know why I have to do it, don't you?"

"Yea, I guess so."

Curtis picked me up and laid me down on his bed. He then walked over and opened his curtains just enough to let in some of the moon light. He looked so good standing there and I was hoping he would lay down with me. But instead he walked over to the bed looked at me and he held out his hand to me.

"You know you have to leave. I can't have you in my room and most of all I can't stand here and look at you. So hurry up and tell me what's bothering you."

I could feel my eyes swell with tears and then I started crying. "Curtis I think that was the cruelest thing anyone has ever said to me."

He took my hand and pulled me into his arms and I could feel his body shake. "No Angela, your taking what I said wrong, I only meant I can't have you here like this when I know I'm not supposed to touch you. Please, you have to understand what this is doing to me."

I went to wipe my eyes but Curtis leaned over and wiped them with his shirt. I could smell his cologne and it smelled so good. As I was breathing it all in, I could feel his warm body as he embraced it to mine. Then our lips met with such passion, I didn't want him to stop. I wrapped my arms around him as tight as I could. I could feel this hands rub over my breast then up the side of my leg as he pulled up my gown. We fell back onto his bed and I felt his fingers go inside my panties and my whole body felt like it was on fire. My body began to arch when I noticed he started to pull away from me.

46

"Angela we have to stop, and we have to stop now. Do you understand what will happen if we don't?"

"Yes, and I don't care. I have loved you for so long and I want to be with you."

I reached out and pulled Curtis back to me and I began kissing him and I could feel him responding back. He slowly moved from kissing my lips to kissing my neck and then down to my breast. As his lips moved on down my body he softly placed his hands on my breast. My body felt like it was going to explode but then we both thought we heard my mom's voice call out. We jumped up so fast and ran to her room where we found her sleeping. We looked at each other and with out saying a word we both went into our own bedrooms and shut the door. It was at that moment I felt so dirty and so ashamed of myself and what I was about to do.

The next morning dad and Curtis were both at the table having coffee with doc. I listened as Doc said; "I don't think Mary will make it to see this winter and if by some miracle she does, she will not survive all the way through it. I am so sorry I wish there were something more that I could do for her."

Dad then said; "Curtis and Angela wait for me here while I show doc out."

We sat there not saying a word while we waited for dad to come back. When he walked into the kitchen you could see he had a heavy heart.

"We all know that your mom has been suffering for many years and I think we are all ready to let her go so she can find peace. Little bit, you know your mother has been hanging on just so she could see you finish school and become a young lady. She loves both of you so very much."

"She loves you too dad." Curtis said as he wiped the tears from his eyes.

No one wanted to eat breakfast that morning, Curtis and I didn't say anything to each other all day. Dad kept himself locked in the bedroom with mom. Curtis and Josh took care of the farm. I cried myself to sleep that night thinking of what dad and the doctor had said. I know dad didn't tell me about mom holding on to hurt me, but all I could think of, was my mom suffering so she could see me finish school and see me grown.

CHAPTER SEVEN

It's been a couple of months since doc came by. All he can do now is make sure mom stays heavily medicated so she's not in so much pain. We still spend time talking to her even though she's not aware of it. Curtis reads to her almost every night. Dad lies by her side with his arm around her. Sometimes I'll see him brushing her hair telling her all about Curtis and me. It's so hard seeing my mom lying in that bed hooked up to all those tubes and IV's. It's really hard not knowing if she even knows your there.

Some days go by pretty fast others drag by so very slowly. It's my birthday tomorrow and that just doesn't excite me anymore. It's just another day without being able to share it with mom. I miss my real dad so much. I want to write him but he won't write back. He stopped writing me years ago.

The next morning I went to see my mother before I left for school and surprisingly she was awake. I called out to her and she looked at me smiling.

"Good morning momma?" I said.

"Good morning my little sunshine, do you know how much I love you?" She replied back.

I was so excited at her awareness.

"Yes momma and I love you too."

Tears were flowing down my face as if I had no control of them.

"I can see you're not my little sunshine anymore. You have grown up so much. I am so sorry to have missed it. Isn't it your birthday today?"

"Yes momma it is, I can't believe you remembered. I have missed you so much."

I fell to my knees at her bedside wrapping my arm around her the best I could with all the medical machines by her.

"I'm so glad I was able to see this birthday. You are a beautiful young lady now."

"Momma I'm almost finished with school."

"I want you to know how proud I am of you and your brother."

"I'm going to stay out of school today so I can be here with you. Let me go get Curtis and Daddy, they'll be so excited to talk to you. I'll be right back and we'll all have cake and homemade Ice cream, Okay momma?"

"Yes dear, that's sounds wonderful."

As I hugged her one more time I could feel her squeezing me just like she used to do when I was a little girl. She pulled me towards her and she whispered in my ear, "I love you now and I will love you forever. No matter what, I will always be there for you; all you have to do is believe."

"I know momma."

"Angela, please promise me that you will take care of your father and brother. You will have to help your father with the farm; he can't do it on his own. I need you to be a big girl and be the woman of the house. Don't let anyone take it away. Will you promise me that?"

"Yes momma, what ever it takes I will do it, I promise."

Her arms went limp as they fell down to her side. I pushed myself upward afraid of what I was about to see. Strangely she was still smiling even though she was no longer breathing. I screamed for Curtis and for dad. Curtis ran up the stairs and when he walked into mom's room he fell at her bedside and grabbed her hand.

"Where's father?" I asked him.

"I think he's in the barn, I'll go get him."

"No Curtis you stay with mom and I'll go. She loved you so much you know!"

"I know she did."

Curtis began to cry out loud as he squeezed her hand. I ran all the way down the stairs and to the barn where I caught my dad and Ms. Amy kissing.

I yelled out; "Dad mom is gone and Curtis is with her now."

Dad pushed Ms. Amy away and as he walked by me he bent his head down and wouldn't look at me. You could tell that he was ashamed.

"I'm so sorry little one, you know I love your mother so very much."

He ran out of the barn and into the house. I just stood there looking at Ms. Amy in disbelief of what I just saw.

"So how long has this been going on between you and my dad?" I said firmly.

"Your dad needed someone and it was better for him to use me then for him to go to you. So you should thank me for that."

"You're one sick lady and you need to get off the farm now!"

"Angela I am sorry you had to see us that way but your father needed someone and it was better for him to turn to me than to you."

"How dare you say that! You better shut your mouth right now!"

"What! Like people didn't know he would go to your room and stay there all night?"

"You're sick, only someone like you would think that way! Not that it's any of your business but yes he comes into my room and no, nothing has ever happened. All he does is talk about his day or he'll lie next to me and cry."

"I'm only trying to protect you and be there for your father. I'm doing exactly what your mother asked me too."

"Don't ever talk to me and don't you ever speak of my mother again."

As Ms. Amy walked through the barn she never took her eyes off me. She stopped at the barn door and turned around. As she grinned so slightly I could tell she wanted me to stop her but I just couldn't nor did I want to.

"Angela you've become quite a lady, but if you and Curtis don't do something fast your dad will lose everything and that includes this farm."

"What do you mean and what do you know about it?"

51

"Honey you need to ask your father and I hope one day you will be able to forgive us. I wasn't lying when I said I was doing what your mother had asked of me. I am sorry Angela, I really am."

Too much was going on that morning to ask dad anything. Doc had helped mom and dad set up pre-funeral arrangements in the way mom wanted it, but a lot of calls still had to be made. That night dad took us into the living room and explained everything. He really had no money left. It took everything he had to care for mom including getting loans on top of loans using the farm and equipment as collateral.

Later that night, Curtis came into my room and said he could hear me crying, I could tell he had not stopped crying either.

"Angela, can I lay with you for a while?"

"Yes, come on and get under the covers it's very cold tonight."

"Angela what are we going to do?"

"I'm not sure right now, I need time to think."

You know dad's drunk downstairs and passed out on the chair."

"Yea, I know. Between losing mom and having to finally tell us about all the debt, I don't know how much more he can take. I do know this much, we need to stick together more now then ever. I'm not sure right now but we'll have to figure it out somehow. I'll find a way, I promise! I promised mom to look after you two and help with the farm. No matter what Curtis, we will not lose this farm."

"I'm sorry I didn't tell you sooner, but I already signed up with the military. I'll have to leave when they call me. I was given a large sign on bonus and gave it to dad so he could put it towards the farm. I also made up my mind, once I get back I'll take over the farm."

"What! When were you and dad going to tell me?"

"I'm sorry Angela. I didn't have a choice the bills were stacking up pretty bad."

"So you knew about the debt way before dad told us?"

"Yes, I found out by accident last year."

Curtis tightened his arms around me and started crying uncontrollably.

"It's alright Curtis. I promise it will be alright."

"The worst part of it all is I'll have to leave you. I think that will be the hardest thing I will ever have to do in my life."

Curtis cried himself to sleep that night while in my arms. I didn't have time to cry I had to find a way to get us out of this mess and some how keep Ms. Amy away from dad.

I didn't get much sleep last night and it's going to be another cold and cloudy day. You could tell that rain wasn't far away. We can't let that stop us we have so much to do. I started coffee and went to check on dad.

"Daddy would you like some breakfast?"

He took my arm and pulled me down on his lap placing his arms around me and kissing my cheek.

"No honey, I'm not hungry."

"How about some coffee I just made a fresh pot?"

He began crying as he held me closer to him. "I loved your mother, you know that right?"

"Yes daddy I know."

"About what you saw, I'm so sorry for that. Will you ever be able to forgive me?"

"Daddy I forgive you and you mustn't think of that anymore, now come on and have some coffee with me and Curtis.

He started stroking my hair and said; "Do you know how much you look like your mother?"

"Thank you, that's a very lovely compliment. Now come have some coffee before we have to get the living room ready for the funeral. People will be getting here soon and we will have to hurry before the rain sets in."

Daddy raised his head up and nodded. We spent the rest of the morning getting everything together.

The funeral went by fine and everyone was so nice. People brought so much food; you could have fed an army. Mom was buried on the property right next to Curtis's mom in a family grave plot. All of Curtis and Dad's family had been buried in that plot. We made it back to the house right before the bottom fell out. All the ladies from the surrounding farms were there to help out. They made sure everyone had a plate of food and they cleaned up afterwards. Once everyone was gone, dad gave Curtis and me a hug and said he just wanted to go to bed and would see us in the morning. Josh stayed at the house that night talking to Curtis and I at least until I finally went on to bed myself.

It rained for three days straight. Daddy said heaven was crying for us and for the grief we were going through. Ms. Amy and Mr. Moore came by the house to give us their sympathy and Ms. Amy asked me for my forgiveness once more. I gave it to her; I guess I knew my dad needed someone and I could only do so much for him. He was going to be a lonely man. He was going to need a female companion and Ms. Amy was a very pretty and caring woman who also needed someone. Ms. Amy and I were close at one time and I'm sure we would become close again. Mr. Moore wanted to speak with dad alone so they went on the porch to talk. I guess they worked out what ever problems they had before.

When Mr. Moore came back inside he came over to me. He gave me a hug and told me how sorry he was for my loss. "You come and see me anytime you want, we can just sit and talk if you like." He said.

"Okay, thank you Mr. Moore."

"I told you my name is Daniel."

Mr. Moore kissed me right on the mouth this time. I wasn't sure how to feel or think about that. He would usually kiss me on the forehead or on my cheek just like all the other men my father knew. He made me feel a little funny inside but in an uncomfortable way. Not the way I felt when Josh kissed me and most definitely not the way I did when Curtis kissed me.

He brushed my hair back and whispered, "What a lovely young lady you have become. I would like to show you the world."

Ms. Amy walked in and asked Mr. Moore if he was ready to go. Mr. Moore gave her a look so fierce that it even scared me.

Curtis and I had been staying away from each other and dad was staying drunk most of the time. I knew he would sneak off with Ms. Amy to the barn. I guess he wasn't ready to bring her into his bedroom yet. He would get drunk and go to Ms. Amy's house or he would go into town where he would stay all night, or for several days at a time. There was one night when Curtis and Josh went to town. They were going to check out a new bar that just opened. I stayed home alone sitting in front of the fire place. All I could think of was Curtis and how I wanted to curl up in his arms. We could help each other with all the pain we felt inside. I know he was hurting just as much as I was from losing mom. I cut the lights out and started watching an old movie when I heard someone pull up in the driveway. I thought it was Curtis so I opened the front door and waited for him, only it was Mr. Moore.

"Oh I thought you were Curtis coming home." I said quickly.

"No it's not Curtis and I don't think he will be home anytime soon. Last time I saw Curtis, he and Josh were pretty plastered. I paid their bill for them and asked the bar keeper to make sure they get a room for the night."

"That was very kind of you."

"On my way home, I thought I better check on you since you were here all alone."

"I'm fine, thank you."

"What are you doing in the dark?"

"I was watching an old movie."

He pushed me to the side and walked into the house and then he pulled me from the door. He shut it, and then locked it.

"Well you don't need to be alone. How about fixing us a drink and we can watch the movie together."

I turned on the lights and walked to the den to fix him a drink but he followed me. He watched me as I poured his drink, when I handed it to him he took the glass and my arm.

He quickly drank the entire drink and asked me, "Where's your drink Angela?"

"I don't drink."

"Have you ever tried one?"

"No and I don't want to either."

"Well I don't like drinking alone." He released me and poured him another. "Here try my drink and if you like it then you can fix yourself one."

"No thank you. I'll pass if you don't mind."

"I said try it. And why are you acting scared of me?"

"I'm not scared of you."

"Then let me fix you a drink and we'll go back into the living room to watch that movie."

He fixed me a drink but I couldn't see what liquor he was pouring. He handed me the glass, took my hand and walked back into the living room and sat down on the couch.

"Drink your drink Angela."

He then got up and turned the lights back off. My heart started pounding so hard I thought it was going to burst right out of my shirt. He came back to the couch and when he sat down he pulled me up against him. He pushed my glass up to my mouth and lifted it. I was either going to drink or drown so I swallowed it. He didn't pull the glass away until it was all gone. It burned all the way to my stomach and I thought I was going to be sick. He put his arm around me and put his feet on the coffee table. The movie started getting blurry and I could feel my head getting heavy and hard to hold up. I knew when Mr. Moore picked me up and took me to my room. He laid me on my bed, and began taking my clothes off. I couldn't move but I could see him smiling at me. I tried to pull away from him but my whole body was feeling heavy. He lay down beside me placing my head in his arm as he started kissing me over and over again. He took his hands and started rubbing and touching my body everywhere. He was telling me what a beautiful body I had and how sweet my kisses were. He then got up and put my gown on me and placed the blankets over me.

"You shouldn't have drunk that drink so fast it went right to your head. You get some sleep now I will lock up on my way out."

I could hear him going down the stairs and I tried fighting the sleep but had no luck.

I woke up feeling a little sick and I had a very bad headache so I slowly stood up and took a shower. When I got out Curtis was there laying on my bed and was ready to tell me about his night, which I really didn't care to hear and I told him to get out.

"Why are you in such a fowl mood? Is it because we left you all alone, is it because you didn't have both of us idiots swarming over you." Curtis replied.

"Okay you can stop right there. If you must know Mr. Moore came over here last night."

"What did he want?"

"Someone to drink with I suppose."

"Oh really, so did you have a drink with him?"

"I didn't have much of a choice."

"Excuse me, but I think you do. What did you do Angela, did you drink with him?"

"He made me a drink and he forced me to swallow it."

"Okay, right. What else did you do or should I say what else did he force you to do?"

"He carried me up to my room, he took off my clothes, and he touched me all over while he was kissing me. The next thing I knew he put my gown on me and left."

"Are you sure you weren't dreaming?"

"Get out Curtis; get out of my room right now."

I pushed him out of my room and locked the door as fast as I could. I stayed most of the day in bed. I was so hurt and angry at Curtis. If he didn't believe me why should anyone else? Mr. Moore could come over here and do what ever he wanted and no one would believe me.

Summertime was here and on this night it was so hot I couldn't sleep, no matter what I did I couldn't cool off. I went downstairs to fix me something cold to drink. I didn't worry about putting a housecoat on. Dad was gone and had been gone since four o'clock that afternoon and

I knew he wasn't coming back tonight. Curtis and Josh had gone back to that bar in town. I thought about going for a swim in the pond but it was too dark for that, so I kept all the lights off and sat in front of the big fan in the living room. It knocked off some of the heat even though it wasn't cool air blowing. I turned the TV on to see what old movie was playing. I haven't done that since the night Mr. Moore showed up. I didn't need to turn on any lights, there was enough light from the moon shining in through the windows for me to get around. Before the movie was over I was feeling much better and was getting sleepy so I cut the TV off.

I was on my way to the kitchen to put my glass up when I noticed the light on. I'm pretty sure I cut that light out, so I slowly walked towards the kitchen. Once I reached the doorway, the light suddenly went out. I couldn't see anything due to the darkness. I was straining my eyes to see something when someone grabbed me! I screamed and hit the person with my glass and the glass broke. I felt this warm liquid in my hand. I heard a man's voice when he screamed and it sounded as if he had fallen. I then realized he had released me so I took off running towards the stairs, when I heard the voice again.

"Angela what's wrong with you? I think you just cut me."

"What! Curtis is that you? I said.

"Well, it isn't Santa Claus." He replied back.

"Well how was I supposed to know it was you? I wasn't expecting you home tonight."

Curtis cut the kitchen light on and I walked towards him to see if he was really hurt. He was bleeding from his head. I guess when I hit him with the glass it broke causing the glass to cut him.

"I am so sorry, come here and let me clean you up. You know it really serves you right for grabbing me in the dark."

Curtis looked at me with blood all over his face and grinned. I have to admit seeing all that blood was scary and I was upset with myself at the thought of me hurting him. After I cleaned all the blood off of him I put a band-aid on the side of his forehead. It didn't really look that bad once the blood was gone.

"Curtis lets go into the living room so I can make sure the bleeding has stopped."

"No." He said. "I would rather go lay down."

"Then lay down on the couch." I said loudly.

"No, I want to lie down on my bed."

"Okay Curtis, come on and I'll help you."

Curtis was so plastered I'm not sure how he was able to get himself home. He said he didn't feel any pain from the cut but he will in the morning. It took all I had to get him up the stairs and into his room.

"Okay Curtis, you need to change your clothes, I will see you in the morning."

Most of the time I feel like his wife instead of his step sister! I walked out and closed the door and as I started to close my bedroom door when I heard him yelling.

"Angela, Angela I need your help."

"What is wrong with you now?" I asked him as I opened his door. He was sitting on the floor leaning against his bed. "Curtis, what are you doing?"

"I was going to take off my pants but I fell back down and I missed the bed."

I started laughing as I helped him back on the bed. I took off his shoes and socks, then his shirt. "Okay Curtis you will have to do the rest on your own."

I started walking away and Curtis reached for me but he fell on the floor again, only this time he began to cry. "Curtis, are you alright?"

"Please stay with me tonight, I don't want to be alone."

"Curtis you know I can't do that."

"Please Angela don't leave me."

I helped him back into the bed and I took off his pants and to my surprise he had no underwear on. "Curtis where's your underwear?"

"Opps I forgot to put them on."

He began to laugh so hard that I started laughing which made him laugh even harder. While we were laughing he pulled me down beside him.

"Curtis, your pants are hanging around your ankles."

He tried to kick them off which just made us laugh even more; finally he was able to kick them off. He was pulling himself upright onto the bed and was pulling me with him until he had us both lying upright on the bed. He pulled the covers over us and he laid his head on my shoulder. "I love you Angela, and if my dad hadn't married your mom I would ask you to be my wife"

I looked down at him and he had passed out cold. I stayed with him for a little while longer running my fingers through his hair. He's so handsome I thought as I watched him sleep. I got up and went into my room. I really wanted to stay with him but I knew I couldn't.

The next morning I wanted to talk to Curtis about last night, only he acted like he didn't know what I was talking about so I just let go. I went on downstairs to find Josh had already made coffee and was sitting at the table with a cup. "Well, did you have a good time too?" I asked him.

"Too good I think; I don't want anything to eat, just this coffee."

Curtis didn't want any food either and as the boys started to go out the door to start work, dad was just coming in.

"I'll be out shortly to give you a hand. I just need to change and get something to eat." Dad said, as he passed by the boys. "I'm sorry little one but will you cook me some breakfast while I go and change?"

"Yes daddy."

He was back downstairs fairly quickly and ate pretty fast. While he was finishing his coffee I poured more coffee into his big cup and handed it to him.

"Thank you honey, I love you and I will see you later."

"Okay daddy and I love you too."

I was so glad to see this day end it felt like it had went on forever.

CHAPTER EIGHT

The phone was ringing early the next morning. It was a man from the military calling and he asked to speak with Curtis. I told Curtis to pick up the phone in the living room and I stayed on the phone in the kitchen. I heard him tell Curtis it was time to report in. Curtis asked if he could have time to get his affairs in order and he was told he had two weeks. My heart dropped as I quietly hung up the phone. I felt so sorry for Curtis; I could tell it was very hard for him to tell dad what they said. What was I going to do without him? Dad told him not to worry about the farm and for him to concentrate on doing what he needs to do. Josh walked into the kitchen and poured himself a cup of coffee. Smiling he said; "What's up with all the long faces?"

"I just got the call to report for duty." Curtis replied.

The smile quickly disappeared from Josh's face. "Curtis, are you serious? Is there anything you need from me?"

"Yea Josh, will you take care of my Angela while I'm gone?"

Dad put his arm around Curtis and said; "Son we will all take care of her, don't you worry anymore about that."

"Yea man, we'll watch over her, don't you worry about a thing here we got it covered." Josh said as he too put his arm around Curtis.

"Thanks Dad. Thanks Josh. I knew I could count on you two."

As Josh and dad were walking out the door, dad stopped and told Curtis how proud he was of him. I couldn't hold the tears back any longer. As I turned away and ran up the stairs Curtis ran after me. I ran to my room and shut the door.

"Angela may I come in?" Curtis cried.

"I'd rather you didn't. I would like to be alone."

"Please Angela, talk to me face to face not through this door."

I opened the door with tears running down my face. I couldn't say a word to him so I turned around and started to walk away when he grabbed me and turned me back around.

"Look at me Angela."

"What do you want from me?"

"I love you, and I don't want to leave you but you knew this day was coming. You knew when we were kids that one day this was going to happen. You knew this is what I wanted to do."

"This isn't fair, that was then and this is now. How can you leave me like this?"

"I don't want to leave you but I have no choice. I already signed up and they already gave me the money to give to dad."

"Let go of me and get out of here. You're a liar and I hate you, do you hear me I hate you."

"You don't mean that and I'm not leaving until you tell me you forgive me."

"Forgive you for what?"

"For leaving you after I told you I wouldn't."

I looked up at him and tears were falling from his face. I could see the pain he was feeling. He really felt like he had let me down. "Oh Curtis, please don't cry. You're doing what you think you need to do and I'm okay with that. I love you more than a sister should love a brother and I know that's wrong but I'm not sorry for it and I never will be."

Curtis picked me up and carried me over to my bed; he sat down placing me on his lap. He placed his finger under my chin and we began kissing.

"I will miss you so much and when I get back if you still feel this way we will get married. I don't care what anyone has to say about it."

We lay back in the bed holding each other as if it were our last time to do so. We kissed and hugged for hours at least until we heard footsteps. Curtis and I both jumped up and started towards the door when dad walked in.

"It's starting to rain." Dad gently said; "Angela you don't have to worry about cooking lunch or dinner. Josh is going into town with me and we won't be back until late tomorrow."

"Okay daddy, is everything alright?"

"Yes, I just have so much to pick up and Mr. Moore will be meeting us there later."

Curtis spoke up and said; "Do you want me to come with you"?

"No son, you just spend time with Angela before you have to go. Now I'll see you two tomorrow."

Dad turned around and headed back down the stairs. Curtis followed him down. I couldn't stop thinking that we were going to have the night to ourselves. This could be the night for us. I was scared and excited at the same time. Is this wrong? If it was, why did it feel so right? Now I'm really confusing myself, what am I going to do? What will Curtis do? For the rest of the day we cuddled on the couch, watched movies, chased each other around the house, talked about everything and we did a lot of kissing.

That night we held hands going up the stairs and Curtis asked, "Your bed or mine?"

I walked to my bedroom door turned around and told him that I was going to take a shower first, and then we can talk about it. I slowly walked into my room closing the door behind me. My whole body was shaking and my heart felt like it was about to beat out of my chest, I had to pull myself together. I quietly cracked my door open to see if Curtis was still standing there but he wasn't. While rinsing out my hair, the curtain opened and Curtis stepped in the shower. I began to shake as he placed his arms around me. All I could do was stand there and watch his every move. He reached for the sponge, soaped it up and started washing my body. I took the sponge from him and started washing him. I could feel my body getting hot like I was running a fever, but at the same time I could feel chill bumps on me as he touched my body. He cut the water off and stepped out of the shower and held his hand out for mine. He wrapped a towel around me and then himself. He took another towel and started using it to dry my hair, then took my hand. As we walked towards his room I stopped and pulled him into mine. We walked inside, he took the towel off me, I took the towel off him and we went to lie on the bed. He was so gentle and slow, he was kissing me all around my face, my lips, he moved down to my neck and I could feel his fingers rubbing all over me. He put his finger inside of me causing my body to bend upwards. He moved from my neck to my breast, kissing me so softly. I could feel him rubbing his body against mine. He took my hand and placed it on his penis and with every stroke I could feel it growing larger and larger. Curtis started pulling my legs apart as he pulled himself upward and over me.

"Angela are you really sure about this?" Curtis said softly.

"Yes, I am. I have wanted you for so long."

With that said I almost screamed when he started to put his penis inside of me. He stopped and very carefully started again, and he was so gentle. It only hurt for a minute. The more Curtis loved me the more I wanted him to continue I didn't want it to end. The heat was building with every thrust as my body ached for more. Our breathing became heavier and the thrusting became faster until it felt like we both exploded into each other. Everything started to slow down as we kissed. He moved behind me holding me tight in his arms as we fell asleep.

I woke up to find us still lying in the same spot. Very carefully I slipped out of his arms and took a shower and got dressed. Once I finished I woke Curtis up so he could do the same.

"Angela. Why don't you lay here with me all day?"

"You know we can't do that, now get up and take your shower."

I went on downstairs to start breakfast. I felt like I was floating on air I have never been so happy. When Curtis came into the kitchen he walked up behind me placing his arms tightly around me. He whispered; "I love you so much my heart feels like it's ready to explode from being so full. You are the only thing I regret leaving behind; I'm going to miss you so much. I want to thank you because if I died tomorrow I would die a happy man."

"Curtis don't you ever talk about dying, I just won't have it nor will I listen to that kind of talk. Although you may repeat yourself on how much you love me."

We were careful to keep things quiet between us and things were going so good. We were so happy. We spent as much time together as we could. We dreaded the day Curtis would have to leave. It had almost been forgotten until the military showed up at our door stop. I felt like my life had ended when I watched him walk out the front door. My heart was breaking as it had the day I watched my father do the same thing. He promised to write me every chance he could and I promised that I would send regular packages from home with every letter I sent back. I cried myself to sleep every night, I didn't want to eat, talk or see anyone for weeks.

Josh wouldn't leave me alone so I finally agreed to walk with him around the pond. Days got easier once the letters started coming in from Curtis. He sent a letter to each of us. Dad and Josh would read theirs out loud on the porch. I didn't dare do that with mine, I wouldn't even open it until I was alone in my bedroom with the door locked. Some days would go by that were more lonely then others. Josh and I would sit on the porch and he tried to get me to talk to him but I couldn't. I didn't dare tell him or anyone else about the feelings Curtis and I shared.

Mr. Moore was coming by the house more and more. I would try my best to avoid him because he was getting very pushy about wanting to take me out. Daddy was no help; all he did was stay drunk and call me Mary. He started spending a lot of time in town. Poor Josh tried to protect me by standing up to Mr. Moore. Josh was doing most of the farm work by himself these days. I tried to help him as much as I could but I had so much to do in the house and in the garden.

CHAPTER NINE

It's been a couple of years now since mom passed away. We were barely hanging on to the farm. Curtis has been gone for a year now. I miss him so much and I can tell dad does too. We get regular letters from him and he sends dad as much money as he can every month. Dad was afraid I would leave him too but I told him not to worry. I would stay and do anything I needed to for us to keep this farm. I had to, I promised mom I would.

Ms. Amy told me that I needed to get out of the house and live a little. She would try to set me up on blind dates but I just wasn't interested. She would even go so far as to bring these men to our home and I would have to get Josh to run them off. Finally I gave in and went on a few dates. I have to admit, it was nice to forget what my life was like for a while, but my heart still belonged to Curtis. Several men asked my father for my hand in marriage but I refused them all. There were even some of dad's old friends wanting to marry me. They went so far as to offer my dad money if they could take me out for a night or if he would let them take me on one of their business trips. Come to find out, they gave him offers like this before when I was twelve. Luckily my dad told them no. When I told dad how sick that was of them, he would laugh and tell me what jokers they were.

Dad and I would sit at the table and talk when he wasn't drinking. He would tell me how much I looked like my mother. After a while he would tell me to go on off to bed because he had some figuring to do. It hurt me watching my daddy trying to figure out what bills he could pay. So far we've been able to keep our heads just above water since mom died. That is until that awful storm came in. It tore up the barn, took almost all the roof off the house, over half of our fields were damaged and killed some of our livestock. I don't know what would have happened if Josh and I hadn't tried to protect as much as we could. I didn't think it possible but dad's drinking got even heavier after the storm. He's stays drunk almost all the time no thanks to Mr. Moore and his homemade liquor.

I notice dad spending an awful lot of time with Mr. Moore and Ms. Amy. I talked to Josh about it and it made both of us very uneasy.

Josh asked, "Do you ever tell Curtis about what goes on here in your letters?"

"No and I don't want you too either. He has enough to worry about without knowing this. Besides Josh, the letters don't come as often as they used to. "

"Yea, I noticed that too. Your dad spends the money he sends faster then it can get here."

"I think it goes to Mr. Moore for that Booze!"

I would catch Mr. Moore watching me every time he was at the house. No matter how much I kept refusing his advances, he continued to push the issue. After Mr. Moore's visits I would have to help my dad up the stairs and into his room. He would tell me how much he really loved me and how he has always seen me as his own daughter. Most nights I listen to him cry his self to sleep and calling out to my mom. I talked to Ms. Amy about this and asked her if she knew what was going on. She explained that my dad was going to lose everything and Daniel was trying to help him save it. Only Daniel doesn't do anything without getting something back in return. She said she couldn't tell me anymore than that.

Several months later at dinner dad wouldn't eat, talk or look at me. I asked Josh if he knew what was going on and he said no. After Josh left, dad said he was going to his room and asked me to come up when I finished cleaning the kitchen. I did as he asked.

"Daddy are you asleep, can I come in?"

"Come on in Angela."

"Daddy what's going on with you? Why didn't you eat your dinner?"

"I just want you to know that I didn't have anyway out nor did I have a choice. I am so sorry to do this to you. But I told Mr. Moore that I would send you over to his house to see him."

"You did what? Why did you do that, and for what reason do I have to go over there?"

"He has been offering to help us and I have been turning him down, but I can't turn him down anymore."

"Why, what kind of offers did he make?"

"Just go see him and he will explain what he wants."

"Okay I will go, but not tonight, I will go in the morning."

"No, you have to be there tonight."

"But daddy it's getting late, why can't I go in the morning?"

"He wants to see you now and as long as you do as he says he will help us. If you don't do it we won't have a home after tomorrow."

"I don't like being alone with him and what do you mean we won't have a home?"

"You promised your mother you would help no matter what, so will you stop questioning me and do as I tell you."

"No! That's not fair and I know what's going on here and I'm not your property to sell. Find someone else to do your dirty work." After saying that, he stood up and slapped me across the face. I couldn't believe he did that. I stood there staring at him in disbelief. He took my arm and pushed me out the bedroom door and shut it. As I stood there in horror with the thought that he would try to sell me. I didn't say anything else instead I went downstairs and ran out the door. I jumped into my dad's pick up truck and headed over to Mr. Moore's house. How dare he use my dad like that, just wait until I get there and give him a piece of my mind.

When I drove up the driveway Mr. Moore was on his front porch. I could tell by the look on his face that he knew I would be there without a doubt.

"Hello Angela honey, how are you tonight?" He had the nerve to say.

"I'm fine sir!"

"Yes you are, come on up here and let me take a good look at you."

As I walked onto the porch I could feel my skin crawl and the hair on my arms felt like they were standing straight up. He was acting as though he just won a prize with his little smirked grin on his face.

"Come here girl and get closer to me."

I started to shake as I walked over to him. He grabbed me around my waist and pulled me down on his lap.

"Let me go, what do you think your doing? How dare you think you can have your way with me! What kind of man do you think you are, trying to use my father in such a manner?"

"Now, now Angela you need to be nice to me if you want me to be nice to you."

"You better let me go if you know what's good for you." Mr. Moore laughed as he said; "Didn't your daddy have a talk with you?"

"I was told to come here and that you would explain it."

"Oh, I see. Well okay then, it's like this; your father needs my help to keep his farm."

"We don't need your help and I'm not my father's property to sell."

"Oh yes you do and so does your family, you all need my help."

"What have you done to my dad? He's not the kind of man that would make deals with you. Most of all he wouldn't have put me in the middle of it. "

"I haven't done anything, I just offered to help and this time he had no other choice but to accept it. Now that's enough talk I have an outfit for you to put on. We will play a game first, okay?"

"What outfit, what game are you talking about?"

"Look it's costing me a pretty penny to have you here tonight so let's get on with it."

"I don't care what it cost you. I choose who I will spend time with, not you and not my father."

"You better listen to me because I will only explain this to you once. We came to an agreement and I paid him quite a bit of money. Part of that agreement included you staying here with me for the night. Your father has enough money to catch up on all his taxes and that is only going to protect him for a little while. He will need a lot more money to cover all his debt."

"Are you telling me that you bought me from my father for the night?"

"I guess that's one way to look at it, so yes I bought you for the night. You belong to me right now so you have to do what I say and with no back talk, do you understand me?"

"You do realize it's not legal and I refuse to do it. You're both very sick men and I'm leaving!"

"I tell you what, why don't you call your dad tell him the deals off. Tell him if he takes the money I gave him to the county, then I will have no choice but to have him prosecuted. Oh yea, when your done with that, may I suggest you go home and get everything packed and moved out of the house right away."

"You can't make us leave our home."

"If your dad doesn't pay those taxes first thing in the morning they will take the farm for the back taxes owed. Tell me Angela where will you and your dad go? What about Josh where would he go? He doesn't have any family left and don't forget about Curtis, what home will he have to come home to?"

He walked up behind me and placed one hand on my shoulder and the other around my waist squeezing. He then turned me around pulling me up to him and looking deep into my eyes. "Have you forgotten about your mom and Curtis's mom?

"What about them?"

"If you lose the farm you will lose both mothers too."

"How can that happen?"

"Both mothers are buried on the farm, are they not?"

"So, what does that have to do with anything?"

"The state will have them removed and placed in the county cemetery."

My eyes started filling up with tears because I knew he was right, I felt trapped. What was I going to do, what could I do? I had no choice but to do as he said. "Alright Mr. Moore you win, but only this time. Enjoy it while you can because you will never touch me again."

"Oh my dear you will want me soon enough and you will find that I am a very patient man and one day you will be my wife. That is, if I decide you're worth keeping."

"Well let me ask you something Mr. Moore, how does it feel to have to pay for someone who doesn't want you back?"

"I'll get my money's worth don't worry. After all you must not forget you just agreed to it as well. So let me ask you, how does it feel selling your body for your step father?"

Without thinking I slapped him so hard my hand print was left on his face. He in returned slapped me so hard, I nearly fell off his porch. I looked up at him and said: "Why do you want me when you can have so many other women?"

"Because I want you, I have wanted you ever since I first laid eyes on you. I want to be the one to show you what making love is all about. I want to be the first one you are with, and the one that will be burned in your memory forever. I want you to want me the way I want you. Do you understand what I'm telling you?"

"Yea, you're a very sick person. What if I told you that you would not be my first?"

He stood there staring at me with fire in his eyes then he began to laugh.

"You almost got me there. Go inside and change your clothes and I will be there in a minute. You will find your outfit lying on my bed upstairs."

I went inside and as I was walking up the stairs I thought I was going to be sick. I walked into his bedroom and on the bed was a black tight fitting mini spaghetti strapped dress with a see through apron, black high healed shoes and nothing else. I wondered if Ms. Amy did this with him and with my dad. No wonder he never married. He only wanted to play house so he could use women for his lust and have no responsibility. I had heard talk that he was in love once and almost married, but I never did find out what happened. I really don't understand why he's doing this to me. He's a very good looking man, very wealthy and powerful. I've seen some of the women he's been with and I've seen others practically throw themselves at him. So why did he choose to torture me? Why is he doing this to my father?

"Angela." Mr. Moore screamed. "You should have been down here forty five minutes ago, what's taking you so long?"

I didn't say anything instead I walked down the stairs wearing this skimpy outfit he laid out for me. I was wondering if anyone else wore it.

"Well look at you, don't you look fantastic."

"I don't know, do I?"

"Come here and let me get a closer look at you. Oh yes, that outfit fits you like a glove, you can see every curve of your body."

"What do you want from me Mr. Moore?"

"First thing I want you to call me Daniel and cook us some dinner. I have everything laid out that I want you to cook."

"You've got to be kidding me, how long have you had this planned out?"

"You'll find everything you need in the kitchen."

He turned me around and slapped me on my bottom as if I were his property. The disgust I felt was unbearable. I felt like I was playing the role of his wife. I cooked his dinner, he ate and he complained because I wasn't eating so I had to eat a few bits to shut him up.

"That was a good dinner. You can go ahead and clean up the kitchen and when you're done how about running me some bath water."

"Is this some kind of joke?"

"I thought we had already gone through all this. I don't want to be forceful but if you continue with this attitude you will leave me with no other choice."

I no longer had anything else to say to him at that point. I could see the look in his eyes and I do believe he could be a very abusive person. I cleaned the kitchen and went upstairs to run his bath. "You're bath water is ready Mr. Moore."

"Stop calling me Mr. Moore. I asked you to call me Daniel did I not?"

"Yes, you did, you're bath water is ready Daniel."

"Good. Come with me and wash my back."

He took my hand and we walked into the bathroom. He locked the door behind us and started taking his clothes off so I turned away.

"Come back here Angela, I need help removing my clothes."

"Please don't do this to me." Tears were forming in my eyes.

"Angela, come on over here to me."

I slowly walked over to him and he took my hand and placed it on his shirt button. I unbutton his shirt and I let it fall onto the floor. I kept my head down so I didn't have to look at him and he took my hand again and placed it on his belt buckle. I unhooked his belt and slowly I pulled his pants down. He raised one foot and then the other as I pulled them off of him. He sat down in the tub and handed me a sponge. I sat on the edge of the tub and began washing his back.

"Take your clothes off and get in here with me so you can really wash me."

"I will not, I can wash you just fine from the outside of this tub."

The next thing I knew he was pulling me into the tub in front of him. I pulled myself back up so I could get out when he grabbed my arm and started squeezing it.

"You need to stop fighting me; you don't want me to loose my temper do you?"

"No, will you please let go of me."

"Only if you do as I say and take off your clothes. I want you to get into this tub with me and I won't ask you again." He let me go and as my eyes were filling up with tears I took off my clothes and climbed in the tub behind him. As I was washing his body I could feel the hatred forming for my father. All I wanted to do was throw up. I was so angry at my father for putting me in this spot. I even felt hatred for my real dad for leaving me behind. Then again, I wonder if my father really knew what Mr. Moore was going to do to me. Surely he didn't; he would not have done this to me. He couldn't have! What if Curtis found out? How would he react? Would he hate his father forever?

"Angela you can get out and hand me a towel."

I got out and wrapped a towel around myself first and then I handed one to him. He dried off watching me the whole time; I reached for those clothes so I could put them back on but he took his foot and kicked them across the room. So I tightened the towel around me and stood in the corner by the sink. He never took his eyes off me while he was drying off and then he grabbed another towel and wrapped it around himself. He took me by the hand and opened the door pulling me towards his bed.

"Okay Daniel that's it, I will not give myself to you freely so you might as well let me go now." He didn't say a word only looked at me and then pushed me down on his bed. I went to jump back up only to have him push me down again. We did this several times until he pulled the towel off me and dropped his towel on the floor. He fell right on top of me pulling my hands up over my head and taking his knee spreading my legs apart. He fell on me so hard that I lost my breath and I couldn't move He knocked the air right out of me. Everything started to go dim and my body was going limp.

CHAPTER TEN

When I woke up everything was a bit foggy. I looked around the room and I realized where I was. The last thing I can remember was Daniel falling on me. I sat up looking for any clothes I could put on. All I saw was a housecoat hanging on the bedroom door so I put that on. I opened the door slowly and looked out I didn't see or hear anyone so I walked down the hallway and very quietly walked down the stairs. I still didn't see or hear anyone but I could smell coffee, so I walked towards the kitchen still no one around. What a relief! I hurried to fix myself a cup, oh it tasted so good. My head was throbbing like a tooth ache and my vision wasn't very clear.

"Good morning Angela." Daniel said as he stood in the doorway.

The sound of his voice caused me to drop my coffee. I grabbed the neck part of my housecoat and turned around to find him smiling at me. I must have had a horrifying look on my face because his eyes had widened as if he were in shock himself.

"I'm sorry for dropping your cup and breaking it but you startled me. I'll clean it up if you tell me where you keep your broom and mop."

"STOP don't you move!" He yelled out.

He was moving towards me and I clutched the robe so tight I almost choked myself. He picked me up and carried me into the living room and sat me down on the couch.

"Stay here I'll fix you another cup of coffee and I'll clean up the mess. You could have cut your feet with all that broken glass on the floor."

I couldn't believe how nice he was being to me this morning. Oh my, what did happen last night? But then again, he does seem to go back and fourth as if he was two different people. Daniel brought me a cup of coffee and went back into the kitchen without saying a word. I drank the coffee and was too scared to move from the couch. Once he came back into the living room he sat down in his chair. He just sat there staring at me not saying a word. His eyes were so kind and soft looking; I couldn't believe this was the same man from last night. I wanted to ask him for my clothes so I could leave. Oh, how I wanted to get out of here as fast as I could, instead I just sat there waiting to see what he was going to do.

A frown appeared on his face and he said; "You look a little confused, are you alright?"

"No I can't remember much about last night. Can you please tell me what happened?

"Nothing happened, if that's what you're thinking. I'm not that evil of a man."

"No, I didn't think you were, it's just everything's so foggy to me and the last thing that I can remember was you on top of me and I couldn't breathe."

"That's because you passed out and once I knew you were okay I covered you and went into the spare bedroom, and that's it."

"Oh, well thank you. If you had done more I don't think I would have known."

"Please Angela, is that the way you see me?"

"You do get a bit forceful at times when things don't go your way. Just like last night you have to admit you were getting a bit rough and I thought you were going to rape me."

"No my sweet one, I would never do that. I told you I am a very patient man and I will wait for you to come to me."

"Daniel I don't want to sound ugly but I will never come to you, I love someone else."

"Well, tell me who would this person be?"

"I can't tell you that, at least not right now."

"Then trust me when I say there will be a time when you will come to me and you will give yourself to me very willingly and freely."

"You seem awfully sure of yourself."

"You will find your clothes hanging in the bathroom. I'm sure your dad will be at home waiting for you."

I was so relieved to know nothing happened and I was happy to get out of there and go home. Although I didn't like being summoned there and then dismissed like I was a whore. Then again, some people may see it as my father pimping me out like a prostitute, after all he was getting paid to send me over here. The more I thought about it on my way home, the more I was getting angry. I am so ready to have a good conversation with my father and he better be ready to explain everything. Once he's done, I will let him know under no circumstances will he ever, ever, do this to me again. If only I knew where my real father was, I would tell him to come get me.

On the drive home I was thinking of how very bossy Daniel was last night, then how very gentle and kind he was to me this morning. Even though nothing happened, I still felt cheap and dirty. I felt that my body, mind and soul had been violated by him and by Brad. When I pulled up to the house I ran inside looking for my father only he was no where to be found. I then noticed a note on the table saying he had gone to the county to pay the taxes, and he knows I will want to talk when he gets back. Fine I thought, at least he understands we do need to talk about all this. I went into the kitchen and started some coffee, before going to take a shower when I noticed Josh sitting on the back porch.

"Josh, I started coffee and I'll fix some breakfast right after I take a shower. Why don't you come on in and sit at the table?"

Josh looked up at me with tears in his eyes and said; "I had to watch over your father last night."

"Why, what was wrong with him?"

"He was going to shoot himself, and you were gone. Angela you didn't come home last night. Where were you? Your father was so worried and he thought you had run away or took off with some man. Why did you worry your father like that? Why didn't you come home last night?"

77

"What! You don't even know what you're saying. He knew where I was, he sent me there."

"Well tell me where you were?"

"My father sent me to see Mr. Moore."

"You spent the night with him? I thought you had better morals then that girl!"

"You need to shut up, just shut up! You have no idea what you're talking about, and you should ask my father what morals he has, not me."

I was so angry at him talking to me that way so I turned around and ran up the stairs. At that point all I wanted to do was take a shower. I felt so dirty for letting Mr. Moore and my dad do this to me. It's my fault too; I didn't really put up much of a fight. I couldn't get Josh out of my head, he was right, where had my morals gone? After my shower and a really good cry I went back downstairs to get some coffee. I saw my father and Josh sitting at the table talking and of course they shut up when I walked into the room.

"Don't stop talking on my behalf. Seems like we all need to talk things through. Don't you agree father?"

"Not now Angela!" My father said. "Just fix breakfast!"

"But dad, we need to talk about last night."

"There's nothing to talk about, just fix some breakfast. Josh and I have a lot of work to do. Some of our worries are behind us now that the taxes have been paid."

"That's great news, how did you get the money?" Josh asked.

"Yes father, tell him where and by all means don't forget to tell him how you got the money. When you're done with that we can all talk about last night too."

"I would advise you not to speak to me in that way Angela. I told you we have a lot of work to do. Josh get up we have to go."

"Stop, you and Josh need to eat breakfast first!"

My father didn't say a word; he didn't even look at me. He just slammed the door as he walked out. Josh was staring at me sadly with such a disappointing look.

In a very rough voice Josh said; "Look at how upset you made your father, you should be ashamed of yourself!"

At that moment I hated them both and myself. I should not have spoken to dad that way in front of Josh. What am I going to do? Dad drinks all the time even while he's working in the field. Josh works this farm as if it were his own. I've seen poor Josh come in for dinner with all his fingers bleeding and he would fall asleep at the table while trying to eat. Several weeks went by without any of us speaking to each other. Daniel had called for me several times but I refused to go and he was starting to get very angry. Dad was starting to get frustrated with me as well.

After a few months went by, dad and I finally talked, but I could tell we would never be as close as we once were. Josh finally let up too, and was being nicer to me. I'll never forget that day as my dad stood in the kitchen doorway. He never once raised his head to look at me while he was talking and he didn't see that Josh was at the refrigerator pouring his self a glass of tea.

"Angela you need to go see Mr. Moore again and this time do as he tells you. You really shouldn't get him so upset."

"What? I will not! You're not my pimp and I'm not your private whore!"

"I'm sorry dear, but we have so many bills and we have a lot of work to do around the farm. Josh and I can't keep doing it alone. I need help and were still trying to fix all the damages from the storm."

"I don't care, we'll find another way. When I promised mom that I would do anything to take care of this family and save this farm, I didn't mean I would sleep with men to do it. Look daddy, I'm pretty sure I can get a job in town. We don't need Mr. Moore's money."

"Angela, Mr. Moore will be waiting for you, and he has asked me to drop you off by 5pm tomorrow."

"You didn't listen to a word I said. Instead you are actually going to take me over there?"

"Yes, I did. We don't have a choice anymore. He told me to tell you that he has a gift for you so you won't need the truck."

"You're as sick as he is! If you would stop drinking so much we might get some bills paid. And how exactly am I supposed to get home?"

"You'll have a ride home don't worry, It's not like I have agreed to let you stay over there. I just need you to help me and your family. If you don't, we will lose everything and both your mother and Josh's mother will be removed from this land. After all didn't you promise to help me and to help take care of this place?"

"Yes I did, but I didn't think it meant letting you sell my body to Mr. Moore. Once he's done who will be the next buyer, father?"

I walked past him and was headed towards the stairs when he grabbed my arm slinging me around to face him. He raised his hand as far back as he could and slapped me. I fell across the chair knocking mom's picture off the end table. I looked up at him as he stood there shaking with such a sad look. I wiped the blood from my mouth and he went straight to the den and started drinking.

I got up and followed him saying; "So is this how you can keep from thinking about what you're doing to me? Is this how you can sleep at night? Is it?"

"Girl, don't start with me right now. I'm your father and you will do as I say!"

"No, you're not my father; a real father doesn't sell his daughter's body to pay for his debts while he's making more debt to buy his booze. You're just a drunken old fool! I'll go, so you better drink plenty. After all you're going to have a lot to explain to Curtis when he gets home."

I wiped more blood from my lip and ran up to my room slamming the door as hard as I could and I locked it. I could hear my dad breaking things and yelling out as loud as he could.

A few hours later my dad came to my door, he was so drunk he couldn't even stand up straight.

"Open this damn door girl or I'll bust it down!"

I screamed back at him, "Go away, I don't want you in here."

He kicked the door open and walked over to my bed where he fell down beside me. He wrapped his arm around me and was crying.

"I am so sorry for what has happened, I never meant for things to turn out this way. Please forgive me Mary."

"Daddy I'm not Mary I'm Angela." I pushed him away. "I think you need to go to your room." He pulled my arms over my head and climbed on top of me. Holding my arms with one hand he took the other and ripped the buttons off my gown.

"Daddy, stop it. Get off me." I screamed as loud as I could.

My breasts were showing from him ripping the buttons off, he took his hand and as he was squeezing one of them he was trying to kiss me. I was kicking and trying to scream as loud as I could. I finally bit his lip and blood went everywhere. He slapped me and pushed the covers down. He pulled my gown up and ripped my panties off.

"Please daddy stop, you don't know what you're doing, Please stop."

I kept begging him to stop but he continued without any hesitation. He kept calling me Mary as he rammed himself so far inside me I thought I was going to be ripped apart.

"Please daddy stop." I begged him over and over.

Only he was getting rougher and rougher by the minute. It felt like it was lasting a life time. My pillow was soaked from the tears flowing from my eyes. My body was aching from the pain of his forcefulness. I couldn't wait for him to get off me as I continued to beg him to stop. He just kept calling me Mary; he thought I was my mother. The alcohol had eaten away at his brain. He finally finished and fell off to the side where he passed out cold.

I climbed out of the bed and locked myself up in the bathroom where I sat in the tub with scalding hot water. I scrubbed as hard as I could, to the point blood was starting to turn my water from clear to pink. My eyes were so swollen from crying and my voice was just about gone from screaming and begging him to stop. I spent the rest of the night downstairs, not able to sleep from the fear he would wake up and come after me again. Finally about five am I went into the kitchen to make some coffee. I could hear Brad was up and moving around upstairs. My heart went to pounding so fast I could hardly breathe. My whole body went to shivering so bad I couldn't hold anything still. Josh opened the back door and I ran to him like a scared little kitten. "Angela, what's wrong with you? Are you alright?" Josh asked me.

I couldn't say anything; I was just shaking so hard he couldn't keep me still.

"What happened here last night?" He said.

About that time Brad walked into the kitchen. "What's going on in here?" Brad said.

Josh spoke up and said; "Why I'm not really sure. Angela jumped into my arms and is shaking like a leaf and hasn't said a word."

I pulled myself away from Josh and ran back to my room. I stood there looking at my bed, seeing the blood from where I bit Brads lip. My body burned with hatred for him. I though going to Mr. Moore would be better then staying in this house. I heard Brads voice, "Angela I miss your mother and your brother, I can't lose this farm too don't you understand?"

"Yes I do, don't you think I miss them too? I will help you as much as I can with the agreement that you stop drinking all that liquor. I think you have had enough after last night."

With a confused look he said: "What happened last night?"

"Are you kidding me? You don't remember what you did? "
The anger was over whelming for me at that point.

"Look at my door Brad. You broke into my room."

"I'm so sorry, why did I do that?"

"You seriously don't know what you did!"

"What did you do to make me so mad that I would bust your door open? You had to have done something to make me that angry."

"So you're saying what happened last night was my fault? How dare you do that! How dare you turn things around and put it on me!"

"Look, I know for me to ask you to go see Mr. Moore isn't what a father should ask of his daughter, but he's a good man. So why do you fight his generous offers?"

"Are you hearing what you're saying? Mr. Moore offers you money only if you give me to him, so he can do whatever he wants no matter how I feel about it. You can't really tell me you don't know what he really wants from me. You know what you're doing; you're selling me to him. Or should I say you're renting my body to him per night. What makes it so bad is he knows he can do what ever he wants and no one will do anything to stop him."

Brad got up with tears in his eyes and walked out of my room not saying another word. I cried myself to sleep knowing what was going to happen and I couldn't stop it either, I wish Curtis was here he would never have allowed this to go on. Later that day I woke up with Josh standing at my bed.

He leaned over me and said: "I over heard you and your dad and I have to apologize for what I had said to you before. I am so ashamed of myself for acting that way, and talking to you the way that I did."

"It's alright Josh, don't worry about it."

"What he is doing is wrong. Angela you can't do it, and you can't go along with this madness."

"You just don't get it, do you? I don't have a choice. If I don't do it none of us will have a place to live. Our mothers will be removed from the property. Tell me Josh where would we go? What will happen to Curtis when he comes back and he has no home, no family and his mother is in the county cemetery? Josh please will you just go, I have to get up and get ready to leave."

CHAPTER ELEVEN

Brad knocked on my door telling me it's almost time to go. I didn't want to move but I knew I had to. I needed something to numb my body, if I was numb then maybe I could block out whatever he has planned for me tonight. I went to the kitchen and got a glass of water and decided to pour some vodka in it. At first I only poured a little, and hey that didn't taste bad so I added more. By the time Brad came back in the house I was feeling pretty good.

He called out and said; "Angela, we better head on out, Mr. Moore won't like it if were late."

"You mean you can't be late handing me over to a man who has plans to rape me. Wow, what a lucky girl I am to have such a devoted father. Tell me dear old dad, what you did last night, was that to break me in for what's to come?"

"I don't need your sarcasm right now. Just hurry up we need to get going."

"Yes dear father. You must keep your end of the agreement."

Neither one of us said a word all the way over to Mr. Moore's house. When we drove up his driveway Brad got out and walked to my door. As he opened it Mr. Moore said; "come along here little girl, don't be shy."

"Please Angela get out we have no other choice."

"No, that's where you're wrong Brad. I for one have a choice and I won't do it."

Mr. Moore walked to the truck and said; "Brad why don't you go on inside and wait for me in the living room, I would like to have a word with Angela. I'm sure we can come to an understanding."

84

Brad dropped his head like a scolded child and went into the house as he was told.

"Now look here Angela, I don't care to have the same problems out of you as I did last time. Now you get out of that truck and come inside with me."

"I have nothing to say to you, and further more, I have not agreed to anything nor will I."

"Get out of this truck with out making a scene and I'll make sure Josh doesn't go to jail."

"Are you crazy? Josh hasn't done anything."

"Okay let me make myself clear. It doesn't matter if Josh did anything or not. If you don't want to see him in jail you will get out of this damn truck, come inside and you will do it right now!"

I saw fire in his eyes and knew he would do something to Josh if I didn't do as he said. Mr. Moore pushed me up against the truck and kissed me while he placed his hand on my breast. "Now be a good girl and go inside so I can talk to your father."

He placed his hand on my bottom and pushed me upwards in front of him. After last night I did not need this. Brad was sitting on the couch, so I sat in the chair away from him. How could he fall into Mr. Moore's traps? Did he ever really love me? Of course he didn't. If he did there's no way he would have agreed to any of this, nor would he have raped me last night. Where's my real dad why hasn't he come to see me? I have to find him, he's my only hope.

"Brad how about a drink?" Daniel asked.

"Sounds fine Daniel. Thank you." Brad responded back.

"Angela, your father and I have some business to tend to we'll be back in a few minutes. Please make yourself comfortable. Come on Brad lets step into my office."

As Mr. Moore closed the door he looked back at me and winked. I felt so disgusted with myself for being there. I thought about how the vodka made me feel so much better. I knew they would be in there for awhile, so I went into the kitchen. I remembered seeing a bottle in the refrigerator the last time I was here. Yep, there it was! I poured myself a glass and drank it. I guess I better mix this with something so they won't know I'm drinking. I poured some orange juice in my glass. When I took a swallow I thought, hey this was pretty good. I refilled my glass with more Vodka and orange juice and went back in to the living room.

I could hear my dad's voice getting louder. What was going on in there, they've been talking at least forty five minutes. Brad opened the door and started walking towards me. He reached his hand out to me. I didn't care to touch him but I thought well maybe this is over. I grabbed it quickly thinking we were leaving but instead he hugged me and whispered; "I'm so sorry little one, I hope one day you will forgive me."

I pushed him away and watched him walk out the door. My body went numb and I could feel this hot sensation all through it. I wasn't sure if it was because he left me, or from me inhaling that drink. I looked at Mr. Moore and he was grinning at me.

"Stay here while I walk your father to his truck."

I fell down on the chair and tears started flowing from my eyes. I didn't have just one father walk out on me I had two. Mr. Moore walked back into the house and I could hear the truck spinning tires down the driveway. I ran to the door, I wasn't going to stay only Mr. Moore grabbed me by my arm and pulled me towards him.

"Oh no you don't, you will be staying here with me. As a matter of fact, you will stay for the next three days."

"Tell me Daniel, how much did Brad charge you this time?"

"Now, now my dear that's no concern of yours; you mustn't worry your pretty little head over such matters. All you need to worry about is me, and do what I tell you. With that we will get along just fine. By the way, since when do you call your father Brad?"

"That's none of your business!"

He grabbed the back of my hair pulling my head backwards. He pulled my body closer to his and started kissing me, and he wasn't gentle about it at all. No, not again I thought to myself. I will not be treated this way; so I bit his lip. He only pulled me in closer to him. He was squeezing the air right out of me. He raised his head with blood dripping from his mouth and said; "If you want to play rough so can I, you better decide which way it's going to be! Why do I taste vodka?"

I began to shake with the unknowing of what was to come next. I tried to twist out of his arms but I couldn't, it felt like he had a death grip on me.

"Angela, I will ask you only once more, why do I taste vodka on you?"

I didn't respond to him so he let go of my waist but tightened his grip on my hair and practically dragged me into the kitchen. He pulled the vodka out of the refrigerator and started yelling; "Are you drinking this?

He pulled me up to the bottle and I knew if I didn't answer him, something bad was going to happen. The rage in his voice was getting stronger.

"Yes, yes I am, so what of it! I have to get something to numb me thanks to you and Brad. The two of you have taken all control of my life and body away from me."

He threw me to the floor and he threw the bottle across the room. He stood there staring at me with this discussed look. I don't know why but that seemed to bother me and for a few minutes nothing was said as I sat there on the floor looking up at him.

"Get up off that floor, clean up that glass then fix dinner. Just for the record I want you for myself but I can loan you out to recollect my money. I don't want a drunken whore in this house, if I wanted that, I would have Amy here instead of you!"

I began to cry as I cleaned up the mess; what has happened to my life? I would give anything if my mom were still alive. I can't stay here, I have to get out. I wiped my tears, quickly cleaned the kitchen and started looking for a way out of the house.

Daniel saw me and said; "What are you doing Angela?"

He scared me so bad that I just stood there shaking trying to think of something to say.

"I asked you a question." He said.

"I have to go to the bathroom."

"Well get on with it and hurry it up, I'm getting very hungry."

I ran to the bathroom trying to think of what I could do. My mind was going in so many directions and I realized there was nothing I could do. If I leave he will pin something on Josh and we will lose our home. It was no use, I was stuck here.

I went back into the kitchen and fixed his dinner.

"Dinners on the table, you better come eat it before it gets cold." I called out to him. Daniel sat at the table and started fixing his plate. He looked at me and I was leaning against the wall.

"Come sit down and fix your plate."

"I'm not hungry." I replied.

"Nonsense, now come here and do as I say."

I sat down at the other end of the table.

"Not there, come over here next to me."

I knew I was definitely stuck so I did as he said. While he was eating his dinner I mostly picked at mine and was wondering what Josh was eating? Daniel grabbed my hand and was looking at me softly.

"I know you're thinking of your dad and Josh but you are not to worry. While you are here with me, Ms. Amy will be taking care of them."

I sat picking at my food thinking of what Daniel had just said. I knew then it was going to be long nights as well as three long days. What plans does he have for me, I wondered? One moment he's kind and very gentle. The next minute he's very persistent and I have no doubt he will take what he wants. My fear is rising with every minute that I sit here with him, while my anger is getting stronger for Brad. I can feel bitterness and disgust building inside for the both of them. Josh knows what they are doing, why doesn't he come and stop all this? I can feel the tears in my eyes but I don't dare allow them to fall on my face.

"Angela that was a fine dinner, I'm going to the den. Tell you what, when you finish cleaning up come find me, I have something to show you."

Daniel bent over and kissed me as if we were really a couple, or was it really to show me he was in control.

While cleaning up I was thinking of what it was he wanted to show me, I'm pretty sure it's a closet of skimpy clothing that he wants me to wear around the house. I have to find a way to protect myself. I looked at everything in the kitchen I knew where all the major knifes were. Just in case I needed to grab one of them very quickly. I started walking towards the living room and was headed for the den when I noticed the front door; all I had to do was walk straight out.

Daniel yelled; "Angela, I'm over here."

He walked out of the den and took my hand. We walked out the front door and around the side to his garage. He opened it and he had a fully loaded black four wheel drive jeep.

"This is for you Angela, What do you think?"

"Why are you giving me that?"

"Don't you like it?"

"Daniel, I'm not Brad, you can't buy me like you buy him."

"Your father needed help and I've been trying to help him for a very long time now. How do you think he was able to afford all that equipment and medicine for your mom for so long? He ran out of money in the second year. Don't you realize without that farm he has nothing and as his friend of many years I will not see him crash."

"You paid for all of my mother's expenses?"

"Yes. Angela, believe it or not but I cared for your mother very much. I couldn't stand by and see her in so much pain. I also promised her that I would help and I would make sure you were taken care of."

"Then why are the two of you trading me back and fourth like a piece of property? I am a human being, I do have feelings and I'm not something you can just use and toss away. Why are you making me pay for the help you gave?"

"Angela no one ever meant to make you feel that way, believe it or not we both love you and I want you to be my wife."

"Love me, I doubt that very seriously, and I can't be your wife Daniel, I don't love you. I told you I love someone else."

"Oh yea, tell me who that was again?"

"That's none of your business and I can't tell you right now anyway."

"Trust me when I tell you that you will learn to love me. I will give you everything your heart desires."

"My heart desires someone else and I will never come to love you. Please Daniel you really need to get over yourself."

He took my arm and pulled me forcefully back into the house. When we got inside he slammed and locked the door, then threw me on the couch.

"Like it or not you are going to be here with me for three days and four nights, so you better get use to it. Another thing, you better start treating me with some respect as well."

He then pulled me up the stairs and threw me on his bed. I was so scared at that point I didn't move as he closed and locked the door. He walked back over to the bed and sat beside me. He pushed me down and climbed on top of me and started kissing me. I could feel my body tremble with fear, I have never been so scared. He looked at me with such anger in his eyes and said; "You will give yourself to me tonight."

"No I won't." I screamed as I jumped up from the bed. He leaped for me as I ran towards the door. He reached out for me and caught my hair in his fingers pulling me back to the bed. He grabbed my hands and arms but I was fighting him and I managed to hit him across the face. That just made him angrier and he hit me; he hit me again and again. He had hit me so much and so hard he almost knocked me out. Blood was pouring out of my mouth and nose. He pulled both of my arms over my head at the same time and handcuffed them together then used rope to tie them to the bed. He started ripping my clothes off and what didn't rip he cut off.

"Please Daniel stop, please don't do this. How can I ever love you after you do this to me?"

He stopped and while he was looking at me I think he realized what he was doing. I could hardly see from the tears pouring from my eyes. He let me go and stood up.

"I'm so sorry; I don't know what came over me. This is not the way I want it to be."

You will give yourself to me freely; I will not take it from you. Please forgive me for this. It will never happen again."

He untied me from the bed and unlocked the handcuffs.

"Please clean yourself up and change into those night clothes; I'm going downstairs for some fresh air."

Daniel walked out of the room and I could hear the door lock from the outside so I couldn't escape. I looked over at those so called night clothes he was talking about. All I saw was a clear lace baby doll night gown that would barely cover my bottom. I had no intentions of putting that on. I walked into his bathroom to wash my face; it was all red and was beginning to swell. I broke down and cried some more. Why has this happened to me? What did I do that was so wrong? I stood there looking at my face, and the more I thought of it the more I realized, I do know what I did. Oh come on who's kidding who? I slept with my step brother and I was in love with him. How much more of a sinner could I be, I deserve everything that's happening to me. I went back into Daniels bedroom and sat on the bed thinking how bad could it really be to give myself to him and to be his wife? He is a very rich and powerful man; and he is a very good looking man. So what's the problem? The problem is I don't love him, I love Curtis. I heard the door unlocking and Daniel walked in with two drinks in his hand.

"Why didn't you change into your night clothes?" He asked me.

"I can't wear that, you can see right through it and there are no panties or anything to go with it."

"Yes I know. I will only ask once more for you to put that on, or I will do it for you. It's your choice."

I picked up the night gown and started for the bathroom.

"Where do you think your going?"

"I'm going to change like you told me to."

"Well you had your chance to change with me out of the room, now you will change with me in the room."

"What! Have you lost your mind? I will not change in front of you!"

"Yes you will, and not only will you change in front of me but you will do a strip tease for me as well."

"You're drunk. I'm going into the bathroom to change."

"Angela you will do as I say or next time I won't stop myself. Now here you go, I brought you a drink it's vodka and orange juice, just the way you like it."

"I thought you didn't want me to drink."

"Once in a while if it helps you to relax and only when I say you can."

"You're some kind of control freak, aren't you?"

"Just take the drink Angela."

I took it and drank it all at once.

"Angela you shouldn't drink like that, it will go straight to your head and you will do things you other wise wouldn't."

"What do you mean by that?"

"Take off your clothes Angela?"

I did become a little light headed and it looked like the room was moving. "I don't think I can do this, something is wrong with me."

"You drank your drink too fast, that's all it is. You have to be careful when you're not used to drinking. Now I will only ask you one more time then I will do it for you, take off your clothes and put that gown on."

Everything started getting blurry. There was something else going on, it wasn't just the drink. I started undressing, first my shoes, my shirt, my pants, my bra and then my panties. I was feeling so strange and so hot, it felt as if I were burning up inside. Daniel got up and walked towards me. He just stood there in front of me staring, and then he took off his clothes. He was placing his hands on me; he was touching me everywhere while he was softly kissing me. The more he did so the more my body reacted to him. It was as if I had no control.

My mind was screaming for him to stop but the words weren't coming out. What's happening to me? Why am I reacting this way? He picked me up and laid me across the bed.

"Do you want me Angela? I won't do a thing unless you tell me so."

My mind was saying no, please no, please stop, but I didn't say anything. I didn't even move. Why wasn't my body responding to my mind? He then proceeded to kiss me. He was pushing his finger inside me and my body was moving as if it was aching for more. I don't understand what's going on. My mind and my body are doing two different things. My vision was so blurry; I was only able to make out the outline of his body. He then pushed my legs up and started kissing my thighs. He slowly moved his lips and tongue downwards. I had never felt anything like this before, my whole body was starting to shiver. He suddenly moved on top of me and quickly took me by pushing himself inside me. It was so fast that it hurt and tears started running down my face, and yet I couldn't move nor was I able to say a word. He went from going fast, to slow, then fast again. It felt like he was on top of me and inside me for such a long time. My mind was crying out for him to stop and to get off me, but nothing was coming out of my mouth. Tears were falling from my eyes. He had to know I didn't want this, but he continued and when he finished satisfying himself he rose up off me.

"I bet that will be a memory you will never forget. I told you that you would want me.

I'm going to take a shower in the spare room; you can use the shower in this room. When you're done put on that gown otherwise you can wear nothing at all. We need to get some sleep I have a long day planned for us tomorrow."

I heard the door lock again as he walked out. My mind was telling my body to get up but I couldn't move, I tried to raise myself up but I couldn't. I was beginning to panic inside. I felt so weak. Daniel walked back into the room and could see I was having a hard time, so he pulled me up and he took me to the bathroom. He cut the shower on and he placed us both inside. I was beginning to feel a little better, but still very weak. After the shower he put the gown on me and helped me back into bed. He placed the covers over me and cut off the lights. He cuddled up next to me as if I were his forever. What plans did he have for me tomorrow I wondered? It didn't take long and I was fast asleep.

CHAPTER TWELVE

I must have slept all night because the next morning I woke up in the same spot. Oh my head, it feels like it's going to split in two. Daniel was already out of the bed and I noticed that the bedroom door was wide open. I put on the housecoat that was hanging on the door and went downstairs; I could smell the coffee and I went straight to the kitchen.

"Good morning sunshine and how are we feeling today?"

"Daniel; do you have to talk so loud?"

"Honey I'm not, you just think I am."

"I know you put something in that drink. There's no way you would have been able to do what you did without drugging me and we both know it."

"You shouldn't have inhaled that drink so fast last night."

"It wasn't just the drink and you know it. What did you put in it?"

"Drink some coffee, you'll feel better. Do you want any breakfast?"

"No thank you all I want is some coffee."

"Okay. Well you pull yourself together while I tend to some business in my office."

"Daniel wait!"

"Yes!"

"I don't want to stay here, I want to go home."

"Honey this is your home as least for the next couple of days anyway. Beside's that's the deal I made with your daddy. Let's just say if you want me to continue to help him and your family, you won't bring this up again."

Daniel walked out of the room and I drank my coffee quietly. My head was hurting too bad to even try to talk to him any further. I could call home but the only phone in this house is in his office. I'll have to wait until I can find time to get in there and use it. I fixed myself some toast to go with my coffee, in hopes it would settle my stomach. Thinking back on last night, I know he put something in my drink but proving it would be impossible. I went back upstairs to shower and change and figured Daniel will be out of his office by the time I come back downstairs. Who knows, maybe I can talk him into letting me use the phone to call home. When I got out of the shower I walked into the bedroom, Daniel was sitting on the bed naked.

"What are you doing?" I asked him.

"Come here to me Angela."

"No, you had your way with me last night because you put something in my drink. I had no control then, but I do now and the answer is no! Now go away, I want to get dressed."

I could see his face turning red when he jumped up and slapped me knocking me to the floor; he then jumped on top of me tearing the towel off my body and forced himself on me again. I was screaming and trying to push him off but it was useless.

"Go ahead scream all you want, no one can hear you and after last night there is no reason for you to ever turn me down again."

I screamed out at him saying; "What is wrong with all you men? You think all you have to do is beat up on a woman to get her to love you, but it doesn't happen that way."

He stopped, he got up and threw some clothes at me and walked out. I reached for the towel covering myself up and just laid there crying.

How can I ever face Curtis again, he can never find out about this, no one can. I'm so ashamed, what am I going to do. These clothes aren't mine they're clothes Daniel got for me to wear while I'm here. This one had a sheer blouse with a mini skirt which had a split all the way up its side. Of course it wouldn't contain any underwear, no bra and no shoes. I looked for my clothes but I couldn't find them any where, he must have taken them away. I bet I could find them in his office. The bedroom door opened and Daniel stood in the doorway.

"Where did you put the bra, underwear and shoes?" I asked.

"You don't need them."

"Yes I do. I want them, where are they?"

"No! I said; you don't need them. They just get in my way. Are you going to get dressed or are you planning on walking around naked?"

I put the clothes on and Daniel took me by the hand. We walked downstairs to the living room. He pushed me down on the couch and handed me a book.

"Here I think you will like this one."

He picked up the newspaper and sat down right across from me in his chair. I for one did not care to read, so I put the book back down on the end table.

"Pick up that book and read it."

"I thought you said you had plans for us today."

"I did. But you wanted to be an ass, so forget it now."

Oh, I can't wait to get out of this hell hole. I have no shoes, bra or underwear, can't exactly take off running looking like this. Even if I could find a way out, where would I go?

"Daniel, is it alright for me to go to the kitchen to get a glass of juice?"

He just nodded his head yes. As I was standing by the sink watching the birds from the window Daniel walked in. He came up behind me pulling my skirt up and over my hips.

"Please don't do this, please stop?"

But he didn't say a word he just pushed me over and took me again like a dog. Once he finished he turned me around and pulled me closer into his arms squeezing me as he kissed me before letting go.

"Angela, I love you and you will be my wife. I will make sure of it."

I couldn't look at him; all I wanted was for him to let me go. He released me and walked out of the kitchen not saying another word. I pulled my skirt down and ran upstairs to clean him off of me. I couldn't even look at myself in the mirror any more. All I could think about was Curtis and how I wish he were here to save me from the repeated rapes. How is he going to react when he finds out what his dad did? I looked again for my clothes but I couldn't find them. I looked in the closet to see if there was something else I could put on but it was empty. I know it was full of clothes before, what did he do with them?

Daniel yelled; "Angela will you come on down here please?"

I went downstairs and into the living room to find him still sitting in his chair.

"What do you want Daniel?"

"I want you in here sitting with me. If you don't want to read you can watch TV." I knew it wouldn't do any good to refuse him so I sat down and turned the TV on. I must have dozed off because I woke up to Daniel saying; "hey there, you need to wake up."

"Oh my goodness, it's dark out, how long have I been asleep?"

"Honey you've been asleep all day. Now come with me into the kitchen, Ms. Amy came by and fixed us dinner."

"What! She was here? Why didn't you wake me?"

"She said you were sleeping so well she didn't want to disturb you, beside's she thought you were exhausted from the love making we were doing."

"What! You know that's not true, you have been raping me repeatedly."

"Raping you, come on now don't be silly. Just look at those clothes you are wearing. Once she saw the outfit she knew way too well what that meant."

"Is that so, well tell me what that means Daniel?"

"Come on, I know you're a bit immature, but I'm sure you can figure it out."

I felt like throwing up. He's going to have everyone thinking that I am here on my own free will, and that I have been sleeping with him non stop. What if this gets back to Josh and Curtis? No use worrying over that now. I'm sure Ms. Amy will pass the word around. I could hardly eat knowing she's going to tell everyone what she thought she saw.

How am I ever going to get out of this, I will have to find a way to make people believe me, but how?

"Come on Angela I'll help you get the kitchen cleaned up. It's late darling and time for bed." Daniel cleaned the table while I washed the dishes. He cut the lights out as we walked out of the kitchen. He walked behind me all the way up to the bedroom. He closed the door and locked it, took my hand and pulled me in towards the bathroom. He decided we were going to take a shower before we go to bed.

Very gently he turned me around and said; "Angela, I can take what I want or you can give it to me. I much rather you give in so I can show you how sweet love making can be. Please don't fight me anymore, give me a chance."

Slowly he took off his clothes and then slowly took off mine. He turned the shower on, took my hand and pulled me inside with him. Very gently he took two wash clothes and soaped them up. He gave one to me and he took the other one. He softly started washing my body. Never taking his eyes off of me, he took one hand to wash me and placed the other on my hand. He pushed my hand around forcing me to wash his body. Once he removed his hand off mine I stop washing him. He grabbed my hand again only this time he squeezed it until I started washing him on my own, then he released me. This is going to happen no matter what I do. I figured if I don't fight him it might go a lot quicker and without pain. So I went along with everything. We finished the shower and he quickly dried himself off, then he dried me off. He picked me up and took me to the bed while he was kissing me. He put me down at the bedside and he climbed into the bed. He held out his hand to me, I took it and climbed into the bed with him. He progressed to rubbing me as he pulled my legs upward. He continued kissing and rubbing me all the way down. My body was getting hotter inside, almost like the first night. Only this time I was able to control my reactions. He was so gentle going inside of me and was gentle all the way through. I was beginning to get confused because I found myself enjoying it. The feelings that I felt were so unreal, one minute I wanted to scream then cry. My body exploded inside, not once, not twice but over and over. Once it was over I was so tired and drained. My body was so relaxed that all I wanted to do was go to sleep. Daniel smiled and put his arms around me. He pulled me close to his chest as the evening drew to an end. For one strange moment I felt secure and safe but with a man I didn't love. How can this be? How can I feel this way? Maybe I don't know what love really is? Maybe I do love Daniel, maybe he had to do this to get me to see it. I don't know what I'm thinking, or what I'm feeling, maybe by morning it will be a lot clearer.

CHAPTER THIRTEEN

Daniel woke me up by kissing me; I opened my eyes and was looking right into his eyes. He had the softest and the gentlest look I think I have ever seen. I could see he really did care about me, so why can't I love him? Perhaps I should try to love him. What am I thinking, I love Curtis? What am I going to do, how can I tell him about all this?

"Angela I brought you some breakfast, with coffee and orange juice. I hope you're hungry?"

"Actually I am; I haven't been eating very much the last few days. Wow that really looks good, thank you."

"I want you to know that I really do love you. I wasn't joking when I told you I wanted you to be my wife. If you agree, I'll pay off all of your father's debt. I will give him the deed to his land free and clear. I'll even give him a very large sum of cash to get all of his help back and get his farm running again. Your father would be on his feet and living the life he was used to before he went broke."

"I can't Daniel. I wish it were that easy, but I don't love you."

"Please think it over. I'll expect an answer by the end of the day!"

"Didn't you hear what I said? I don't love you Daniel."

"Your father will lose everything by the middle of next week if you don't say yes. I'll leave you alone to think about it. I must have an answer no later then tomorrow morning."

"Are you not hearing me? I can't marry you; I don't want to marry you!"

"No, I think your not hearing me. Either you marry me or your family will be on the street. Your mother and Curtis's mother will be removed from the property, and Josh will spend the rest of his life in prison."

"Are you trying to force me into marring you? Why of course you are, that's the only way you know how to get what you want."

"You will have to do this willingly and without anymore questioning. Don't force me into making a call that could put an end to your father and Josh. Now my patience is wearing very thin right now, so you better give me an answer soon."

"Okay I'll do it, but I need to go home just long enough to talk to Brad. I promise I'll be back tonight."

"I believe you. There's an outfit in the closet for you to put on."

"What kind of outfit?"

"Don't worry it's a nice outfit that you can wear out in public."

Daniel took my tray and sat it on the floor. He took off his robe and climbed on top of me. "Angela I love you and I will do anything and everything to make you happy. I'll help your dad get back on his feet and I'll even get him to stop drinking. I'll make sure he moves on with his life, which will be easier once he's financially sound."

"Daniel, don't you see what you're doing to me? You're forcing me into this marriage and this is not the way to get what you want. I don't know what I did to make you want me so much, but making me marry you isn't going to make me love you."

"I told you I was in love with somebody else. I can't be in love with two men at the same time?"

"I know you said you love someone else but you won't even tell me who. All I can tell you is he will never love you as much as I do or in the way that I can. Honey, once we are married everything will change for the better for so many people that you care about."

"I would like to see Brad and I would like to talk to my brother. I want to be the one to tell them."

"Angela, I want to do as you ask but time is running out for your dad even as we speak. Your father is in debt to just about everyone in the county. He's so far behind on all of his payments and everyone has refused to give him any additional time. If he doesn't get them paid soon, they will take it all. Your mother and Curtis's mother will be removed and placed in the county cemetery. They will be placed without any acknowledgment of who they are. Now tell me Angela, is this the way you want it all to end?"

"No, of course I don't and you know that."

"All of it can be stopped today. You have the power to do that. All you have to do is leave with me today, right now."

As I laid there in Daniel's arms I knew I had no other choice and how bad could it be, Daniel would love me and he would take care of everything. My family will be able to keep the farm, Brad will get help to stop drinking, and Curtis and my mother will remain where they are. Josh will be safe and Curtis will have his home to come back to.

"Angela if you say yes to me right now we will leave this afternoon and I will make the calls to have your dad taken care of."

"How long are we going to be gone and where are we going?"

"I know a really nice place where we can get married, and then of course we will have to go on a honeymoon. I'll get everything set up; all I need from you is yes."

"Daniel I had always thought I would have a wedding like my mother's when I got married."

"We can do that later, or if you want, we can do that now but I won't do anything for your father until you are my wife. So which way will it be Angela?"

"You really aren't giving me a choice. I'll do it, but can I at least talk to Brad?"

"We won't have time. I'll send word and you can call him later."

"Alright fine, but where are we going?"

"Sorry dear but that's a surprise; now pack your bag while I make some calls."

"How do I pack, for warm weather or cold? Oh wait, I have no clothes to pack."

"You know what, don't worry about it. I'll buy you all new clothes once we get there, just get dressed so we can go."

Daniel ran out of the bedroom with so much excitement and I sat on the bed wondering; what am I about to do? My head is spinning in so many directions right now, I can't even think straight. I need to talk to my family; I want and need to talk to Curtis. How can I just take off and do this without talking to him first. What is he going to do when he finds out? I have to find a way to tell him and make him understand that I have no choice. My heart dropped when I heard Daniel call out.

"Angela. Honey you need to come on down it's time to go."

As I looked in the mirror I could only imagine what this was going to do to Curtis. Slowly I walked down the stairs. I was trying my hardest to keep the tears back and the images of Curtis out of my head. Once I got to the bottom of the stairs Daniel was telling everyone to keep working, and to watch out for the place while we were away. We should be back in a couple of weeks.

"Daniel, do we have to be gone so long?"

"Honey, don't worry about that. I've got all the arrangements made. All I need for you to do is stay by my side and look pretty."

I could feel my blood boil when he said that, oh he really knows how to degrade someone. How can I do this, I should run. His mood changes like day and night, I have to stop this. I have to do this if I don't my whole family will lose everything. Not to mention that they will dig up both Curtis and my mother and move them to who knows where. I just don't understand why we have to stay away for so long? What's Daniel up to now? Daniel took my arm and we walked out the door towards the car.

"Daniel you're squeezing my arm and it's hurting me, please let me go? You don't have to keep pulling and tugging on me like this. I already told you I would marry you, what more do you want from me?"

He didn't even bother to look at me; he just pushed me into the back seat and shut the door.

Daniel stood outside the car talking to the driver, the driver nodded as he re-opened the door for Daniel. None of us were saying a word, but I noticed we didn't get on the main road. We were still on the property driving through some woods into an open field, where a plane was sitting and waiting for us. The driver told Daniel his plane was loaded and ready for take off. I don't believe it, Daniel owns this plane. What doesn't this man own, who doesn't work for him and what does Daniel really do for a living? As we got out of the car Daniel kept one hand on me at all times. It was like he knew I would run if I ever had an opening. Once we loaded the plane he checked to make sure I was strapped in before he went to the front. Within minutes the plane started taking off only Daniel never came back to where I was sitting. Once we were in the air I got up to see what Daniel was doing. Heck for all I knew he may not be on this plane, but he was, he was the pilot!

"Daniel what are you doing?" I asked him.

"Angela my love, how's your flight so far?"

"Fine, but what are you doing?"

"This is my plane so what do you think I'm doing? We have to make a little stop before we can go any further.'

I watched him fly the plane with such confidence; Daniel has that if nothing else. This is a man who is very sure of himself.

"Honey." said Daniel. "I must ask you to please go back and sit down. We are going to make a quick landing."

Confused, I went back to my seat, not sure of what to expect next. He landed the plane and I stayed in my seat not sure if I was to move. I tried to look out the window to see if I could see what was going on. Daniel walked over to me and very quickly unhooked the seat belt. He took my hand and we walked off the plane. It looked like we had landed in a field. I pulled from Daniel just a bit when I noticed a handful of people standing around talking. They were acting as if they had been waiting for us. Then I noticed a man who appeared to be a preacher with two ladies standing beside him. The two ladies were holding flowers and behind them were several other men all smiling.

They were all very excited to see Daniel and as we got closer Daniel said; "Hello Preacher this is my Angela!"

"Well hello Angela, I have heard so much about you. Over the years I have asked Daniel to bring you over for us to meet but he always had an excuse. I was beginning to believe that Daniel had made you up, until he notified us of this wonderful news."

Confused I replied; "Wonderful news?"

"Yes, I was very happy to hear of you accepting his proposal. Angela, this is my wife Suzie and our daughter Helen. They will stand in as witnesses and here are your flowers."

All of this had stunned me so much, I couldn't say a word. How long has this been planned? I wanted to say something, but I just couldn't get it out of my mouth. The preacher began the service, which was very quick and short. Daniel said his I do's and then it was my turn, only nothing came out, I just stood there.

The look on Daniels face was very haunting when he said; "Please excuse us preacher but Angela's a little over whelmed and I just need a moment with her."

"You go right ahead my son, this happens from time to time."

Daniel took my arm and pulled me back towards the plane. I could tell from the squeeze he had on my arm that he was getting angry. The pressure was becoming so intense my arm was starting to go numb. We walked around to the other side so no one could see or hear us. He pushed me into the side of the plane so hard the back of my head hit against the plane.

"Angela what are you doing? You're embarrassing me."

"I'm sorry; I just froze and couldn't say anything. But if you really want me to be honest here, I don't think I want to go through with this."

"Angela you do want to do this and you will do it."

"Daniel, what is wrong with you? You change moods faster then I can blink."

"Get your ass out there and say I do, because if you don't, your daddy will be out on the street and in jail before you can turn around good!"

"How can you live with yourself making me marry you by making threats against my family? You just wait until Curtis gets back home. When he finds out what you are doing to me, he'll come get me. He truly loves me and his love isn't like your so called love."

"Curtis! Your brother Curtis! That's who you're in love with? What the hell is wrong you? Do you know you can both go to jail for that?

Do you know he could get a dishonorable discharge for that? Do you know people would turn their backs on your entire family in disgrace if they knew this? Tell me Angela, is that what you want?"

"No! No I didn't know all that, and No, that's not what I want. Daniel, you mustn't tell anyone please."

"I won't tell because I still love you. That's the kind of love I have for you. All you have to do now is get back in front of the preacher and say I do. As long as you do that for me, I will keep your dirty little secret. And as a bonus I will still take care of your family for you."

"Alright Daniel, you win! I will do as you ask. You have me; you have all of me now. Just please help my family and don't hurt Curtis"

"Okay Angela, fair enough. Take my arm and let's go back and get this done."

I took his arm and we walked back towards the preacher, I never felt so alone and ashamed in all my life. I now belong to Daniel. I was his property no matter how you want to look at it; I was his for as long as he wanted me to be. Once I do's were said, Daniel put a ring on my finger that had a diamond so big it almost covered two of my fingers. Oh yes, it was beautiful, but for me it was the lock of death. From this day on my life was over. My future with Curtis was over as well. The one true love of my life would be no more. Daniel and I walked to the plane and he told me to sit down and strap in. He walked back towards everyone outside. I watched him from the window shaking hands and laughing with everyone. I leaned back in my seat wondering what my life was going to be like with Daniel. I don't have to guess, I know how it will be. I'll be his puppet to do as he says and to react to every little desire he has. I just wanted to die; at least death was better than living a lie with him.

I must have dozed off, because the next thing I heard was Daniel calling out to me.

"Angela darling we're here, get up and come see your new home."

I didn't say anything when I walked off the plane. We had to walk across this long bridge from the water to the Island. Water was all around us and I couldn't see anything else. Once we topped the hill I saw what appeared to be a lodge of some kind. As we got closer it was looking so lovely and very romantic. I would bet couples that were in love would come here to be alone. Once inside it was quite a site to see. Then the real truth came out of the devils mouth himself. "Angela there is one more thing that I want from you! We are going to stay on this island until you have conceived because I want a son right away."

"What! Just like that you want a child from me? What if I don't want to have a child with you? Did you even consider that we might have a girl instead of a boy?"

"Yes Angela a child just like that, or for as long as it takes. As far as if you have a girl first well, I guess that would be fine and we'll just continue until I have a son. I need a son to carry on my legacy. Get settled in and take a look around, it's a beautiful place here. I'll be back in a couple of hours. I have some business in town to take care of. I don't want you to worry about dinner tonight; I'll bring something back with me."

"Are you going to leave me here all alone in the middle of no where?"

"You'll be fine I'll be back as soon as I can, don't worry."

"But Daniel, there's no phone, what if something happens?"

"I said you'll be fine. I'll see you in a couple of hours."

I watched Daniel leave from the big bay window. Once he was out of site I went through the entire place. I thought there had to be some way to communicate with someone and maybe figure out where we were. But I could find no TV, no radio, only a record player! Although it was stocked with food, water, medical supplies and anything else we may need. I found clothes in this huge walk-in closet but they were mostly stripper to loose fitting items and nothing else. I went back to the living room and began to cry like no tomorrow until I cried myself to sleep.

CHAPTER FOURTEEN

"Angela, honey wake up I brought us some dinner back."

I got up and followed Daniel into the kitchen. He had everything laid out on the table. He even had a vase of flowers in the middle of the table with candles on each side. The lights were dim and he had soft music playing in the back ground, it was so romantic.

"Daniel this is so beautiful."

"Now that you're my wife this is the way it will be for you all the time. This is the life I want to give you; all you have to do is just open up and let me in. No one will ever love you the way I do, no one."

Tears slowly started falling from my face. Daniel wiped them away saying; "Oh no my love, there will be none of that."

As we looked into each other's eyes he took me into his arms softly kissing me. For a moment I felt like I was in Curtis's arms. As I thought back to when Curtis was kissing me, I began kissing Daniel back. Daniel picked me up and carried me to the bedroom where we made love to each other in a way we have never done before. I kept my eyes closed as I kept thoughts of Curtis in my head. The vision of him was so real in my mind that I could feel Curtis touching me and kissing me. I didn't dare open my eyes in fear I wouldn't see him. When it was over Daniel was lying behind me holding me in his arms.

You could feel the heat from our bodies touching and for a moment I felt so safe and contented. Then I heard Daniel say; "I love you Angela."

Before I could even think I blurted out; "I love you too Curtis."

Daniel's voice became very stern when he said; "What did you say?"

He turned me over so he could see my face. I too was shocked at what had come out of my mouth, but it felt so real. It felt like I was with Curtis not Daniel. The look in Daniels eyes was horrifying, what am I going to do? If I don't say something he might kill me right here.

"I am so sorry Daniel. I just have my family on my mind so heavily right now, and you didn't even allow me to say goodbye."

"Get up." Daniel yelled out as he jumped out of the bed.

He yanked the covers off of me and threw them in the floor. I was scared for my life I didn't know what he was about to do next.

"Get up." He said again.

I got up and stood there in front of him totally naked. I was shaking like a leaf as I tightened my body up and waited for him to hit me.

"Angela, you just ruined a perfect evening, how could you do that? This was between you and me, how could you bring him into it? What's wrong with you? Don't you care about anyone else besides yourself?"

"Daniel I am so sorry, I don't know why I said that."

"Tell me you love me and say my name."

I stood there shaking and so scared that my voice quivered as I said; "I love you Daniel, I love you."

Daniel grabbed the back of my hair pulling my head backwards. With my head bent backwards I found myself looking right into his eyes and thinking how he could literally break my neck right now. As I begged him to let me go, tears were starting to rush down my face. He threw me on the bed and walked out of the room. Oh what have I done? He will find a way to make me pay for this I just know it. I got up and was gathering the covers when he started calling for me to come back into the kitchen. I didn't even bother to put my clothes back on; instead I grabbed a house coat from the closet and went to the kitchen.

"Why don't you warm up our dinner, I'm hungry. I tell you what; once we eat you can show me how much you love me and only me."

I warmed up our food and we ate in total silence. It was so quiet you could hear the ocean hitting the rocks. When we finished dinner, Daniel got up and went back towards the bedroom. I stayed in the kitchen and cleaned up the dishes. I was trying to get myself mentally ready for

Daniel. I walked into the bedroom to find the lights cut off. The music was playing and candles were burning all around the room. I went to take off the house coat and climb into the bed, when Daniel stopped me.

"No Angela stop; don't take that off yet. I want you to say you love me. I want you to look at me while you say it. Do you think you can really do that?"

"I'm going to try, but you can't really expect me to be in love with you. You make me do everything your way! You didn't give me the proper time to really know you. You didn't even give me a chance to fall in love with you in the right way."

Daniel sat up and said; "Come here to me."

I walked to the side of the bed and as he pulled me closer he said; "I'm so sorry Angela, but I was afraid I would lose you if I didn't act right away. I need you, don't you understand that? No one but my doctors know what I am about to tell you. I have an illness and there's no cure for what I have. They can't say for sure how long I have. It could be years or it could be months, the doctors don't know. Trust me when I say I have gone to the very best of doctors. So you see; I need a son to take over my business. I need a wife that will love and take care of me and I wanted it to be you. I'm sorry that I didn't give you a chance to choose me."

He placed his head against my stomach. My heart was crushed for him as tears fell from his eyes. No wonder this man has so many mood swings. He has so much to deal with and he has no one to help him through it, no one but me. I know what it's like after having gone through it with my mom. I slowly pushed Daniel from me and I took off my house coat. As our eyes locked into each other I pushed Daniel backwards on the bed. I climbed on top of him and I kept my eyes open and on him so he could tell I only had him in my thoughts. As I began loving him he started loving me back, we made love to each other and there was nothing or anyone between us. I truly gave myself to him unconditionally. I felt like I was finally starting to understand this man, and he needed me. I could also see why he felt he needed a son. I'm sure one day I will fall in love with him and hopefully it will be before he passes away. I will give him what he wants and what he needs. I know our child will be well provided for. I guess I should feel honored that he chose me; to the point he would take care of my whole family that has to be love. He has to love me to do that.

CHAPTER FIFTEEN

We have been on this island for almost three months now. Daniel had several pregnancy tests in the house and he would test me weekly, until the day it showed positive. In what we believed to be my seventh month, Daniel decided we could go into town to live until the baby was born. I was upset because I wanted to go home.

"Daniel please, can't we go home? I want to have the baby there with my family, Please?" Daniel didn't say a word as he loaded the plane. Once he was finished, he helped me inside and very gently strapped me in. He softy kissed my lips and went to fly the plane. I knew Ms. Amy had already told everyone about Daniel and me. Curtis should be at home now and it's him I will have to face. Not only about marrying Daniel, but now I'm going to give birth to his child. Daniel landed the plane in what appears to be a landing strip.

I heard Daniels voice over the intercom; "Angela stay here and I'll be right back."

It didn't seem to be long at all when Daniel walked over to my seat and before he could say anything I spoke up and said; "Daniel I really want to have this baby at home."

"Angela you do love me now don't you? I mean, you have to right? We've been alone for almost a year and you're going to have my baby. This should have changed everything."

"Daniel I do care for you. You said I would grow to love you and in some ways I guess I have. You also knew I was in love with Curtis and that will never change."

"You will love me, you do love me. Will you tell Curtis you don't want anything to do with him? Will you tell him that you're in love me?

113

Most of all he'll have to see you're telling the truth, after all your going to have my baby. Or if he can't understand that then I can always have him killed?"

"What! You have to be joking, you can't be serious?"

"Angela, do I look like I'm joking? You will do as I say, do you understand me?"

"Will you please stop it Daniel, I'm not going to leave you. I gave myself to you and we are going to have a baby. This child will need his mother and his father for what ever time that may be. I do love you, so please I don't want you to behave this way anymore. You don't need to fear Curtis either. I'm not going to run to him, I'm going to stay with you."

"So you do love me?"

"Yes Daniel I do."

"Alright Angela, I'll trust your words for now."

Daniel left to go back to the front and as we were flying all I could think about was how jealous he was. He's so jealous of everything that he owns and that includes me and his baby. I truly believe he would have Curtis killed at just the thought of me leaving him for Curtis. Daniel knows how my heart aches for Curtis. He also has a very high temper and he knows so many people. He can do what ever he wants and I'm proof of that. Daniel never did give me an answer on us going back home. I looked out the window and noticed we were landing on Daniel's opened field. Then my mind started wondering; why has he done this? What is he up to? I was excited to be home and yet I was scared to death. I know he has something up his sleeve; you can't live alone with someone and not learn a little about them. I learned that he is capable of doing anything. As Daniel walked towards me in the plane I could feel my skin crawl, I knew something was wrong. I had this feeling something was about to happen, and I'm afraid that I'm going to be in the center of it.

"Come on Angela, we're home just like you asked for. I love you enough to bring you home to have our baby. Just make sure you keep your part of the bargain and keep your distance from Curtis."

"But you know I will have to face him now that we're back. I'll have to explain about us and this baby. You know he'll have a lot of questions and if I don't answer them he will never leave us alone."

"Okay, you're right. Tell him what you have to and make sure he understands that will be the end of it. Now come on your family is waiting at the house for us. I really hope you make yourself very clear and they understand you are with me and nothing will change that."

"Oh thank you Daniel, you'll never regret this I promise."

My stomach went into knots at the thought of seeing Curtis again. Daniel's driver was there with the car waiting for us as we got off the plane. I was getting nervous as we got closer to the house, I felt like I was going to throw up. My heart started racing and I was shaking unbearably as we drove up the drive. I could see Curtis standing on the porch talking to Josh. My heart started beating so fast that you could see my shirt move. The driver drove around the side of the house to the garage. When the car stopped, Daniel stepped out and reached for my hand to help me out. I saw Brad and Ms. Amy running towards me and Brad was calling out my name as he was crying; "Angela, Angela my little one, I have missed you so much."

"Hello Brad." I replied very coldly.

Brad stopped in his tracks and as he looked at me he said; "Angela, Oh my goodness, just look at you."

"Are you sober?" I said.

"Yes, with Daniel's help." Brad said proudly. "Daniel paid for everything; I went into therapy and had help with treatment. I had a lot of help to stop drinking and I now have everything back. The farm is running smoothly and I'm making money again. Honey, we owe him for so much, he saved this family. I want to thank you for everything you did to make all this happen. I explained everything to Curtis; he was pretty upset at first. When he came home the first thing he did was run through the house looking for you. Angela honey, I didn't know the two of you were in love with each other. If I had known I never would have let things go the way they did. Will you ever be able to forgive me?"

"Did you tell him everything that you did to me? Did you tell him how you took me? Did you tell him how you sold me to Daniel? Did you tell him the real truth or only enough to make him hate me while he felt sorry for you?" I said in anger.

About that time Daniel spoke up and said; "Okay, that's enough from you Angela. Brad you also need to walk away, I don't want Angela getting upset; she needs to go inside and get settled."

"Daniel, I need to know what he told Curtis. How can I talk to him and get him to understand if I don't know what Brad said?"

"Angela I don't think it matters anymore, does it? Besides if you tell him that Brad sold you to me then how is that going to make me look?"

With the look Daniel gave me I didn't dare say another word. I turned around and started walking towards the house. Daniel reached out for my arm, I pulled it away from him, and he huffed and reached for me again. He squeezed so hard it stopped me right in my tracks.

"Listen to me because I'm only going to tell you this once. You need to calm down and remember what I told you. You are in love with me and you are about to give birth to my child. Just so I make myself very clear, this child belongs to both of us. So if you don't want to lose your rights you better stay clear of Curtis. Now with that said shall we go into the house? You can see the rest of your family before we have to ask them to leave. You need your rest or do I need to ask them to leave before you even get inside?"

"No. I'm sorry Daniel. Please walk me inside."

Daniel and I walked inside the house and when we walked into the living room there was Curtis. "Angela!" Josh cried out as he ran to hug me. "Look at you, are you alright? You've been gone for so long and we've really missed you."

"Hello Josh, I missed all of you too. I'm estimating myself to be about seven months."

Josh looked at Daniel as if he could run right through him. I was trying to look for Curtis without letting on to Daniel. About that time I felt someone touch my arm and I jumped thinking it was Daniel. Only it was Ms. Amy.

"Hello dear, you are absolutely glowing."

"Thank you Ms. Amy."

A very strong voice spoke out. "Have you seen a doctor?"

I looked up and Curtis was walking towards me. He looked so handsome and yet so broken. He opened his arms and I couldn't help myself as I ran right to him.

"No I haven't, not yet anyway. Oh Curtis it's so good to see you."

"I've missed you so much Angela, I didn't understand why you weren't here when I came home and why I didn't hear from you. You could have told me about you and Mr. Moore before you just stopped writing to me."

"I'm so sorry Curtis, I didn't have a choice. Besides your letters started slowly down and I'm sure you didn't tell us everything either."

"What do you mean you didn't have a choice? I wrote as often as I could."

Daniel spoke up and said; "She didn't mean she didn't have a choice, it's just that everything started happening so fast. We just got wrapped up in the moment and shoot before we knew it this little girl and I took off and got married. As you can see it's been pretty productive, we are expecting our first child pretty soon. As far as seeing a doctor, well he's on the way as we speak right now. My baby wanted to have our baby here at home with family and friends. Well, come along now Angela, it's time to go upstairs and lie down, it's been a long day for you and the baby."

Daniel took me by the hand and by the waist pulling me away from Curtis. Once we reached the stairway he bent down kissing me in front of everyone. I guess that was really for Curtis's benefit.

"Please excuse us everyone but Angela needs to lie down until the doctor gets here. Thank you for coming and if you will, please see yourself out. We'll have to get together again real soon." Daniel had my view blocked so I couldn't see anyone but I could hear them leaving. I did over hear Curtis tell someone that he was happy for me. If only I could tell him the truth, if only he really knew what was going on. My heart is breaking all over again and I don't dare let it show in front of Daniel.

CHAPTER SIXTEEN

We walked into the bedroom and Daniel said; "Angela you need to lie down and get some rest. I'll bring the doctor up when he gets here."

I agreed with him, I was pretty tired. I changed into a nightgown and climbed into bed. It had been a long trip home and it was good to see everyone.

"Would you rather I stay with you until the doctor shows up?" Daniel asked.

"No. But thank you for thinking of me. I just want to lay here and go to sleep I'm really tired."

"Alright I'll go back downstairs and wait for the doctor. I love you Angela."

Daniel walked out and closed the door. I could feel tears running down the side of my face onto my pillow. I couldn't get Curtis out of my head I was wondering what they really told him. He looked so unhappy and it's my fault. I know they didn't tell him the real truth. I have to find a way to see him so we can talk, I need his forgiveness. Oh, I just can't think anymore I am so tried. It felt like I had just closed my eyes when I heard Daniel talking to someone outside my door.

The door opened and Daniel asked; "Angela the doctor's here to see you, are you awake?"

"Yes Daniel I am. Hello Doctor, thank you for coming out here to see me."

"Hello Angela, Daniel tells me you haven't seen a doctor yet. I was just explaining to him that wasn't very smart considering you could be seven months along. You and the baby needed medical attention from the very beginning."

The doctor laid his bag down by the bed and looked up at Daniel and said; "Sorry Daniel but I'm going to have to ask you to wait outside. I'll let you know when you can come back in. I'll need to check her to see if everything's alright and to see how far along she actually is."

You could tell by the look on Daniels face he didn't like being dismissed. Luckily he did as the doctor said and didn't respond back. Mean while the doctor did his thing, he took blood, examined me inside and out without really saying much.

The Doctor picked up the chair and placed it next to my bed. He took out a folder and opened it as he sat down. He took a few minutes documenting everything. He started asking me so many questions about where we were, why I didn't see a doctor, why I didn't stay in touch with my family and he just went on and on. I was scared to give him honest answers, but for some reason I explained everything the best way that I could. I told him everything that led up to this very moment and I could tell he wasn't very happy with what I had to say. I asked him not to say anything to Daniel or he would explode. I explained that Daniel could be a very dangerous man.

"Angela you and the baby seem to be doing fine, although you do appear to be eights months along instead of seven. As far as me repeating anything to Daniel I really don't want you to worry. Anything you talk to me about will stay between you and me and no one else. You seem to be under a lot of stress right now and you don't need anymore added to it. I must say that I don't think this is the best relationship for you. I remember when we were in school and my dad took care of your mom. It broke his heart that he wasn't able to cure her cancer. I remember him telling me that he had promised your mother to watch over you. I must say Angela; I too found it a bit odd that you left the way you did. You didn't say anything to your dad that you were leaving. Your dad seemed to be so devastated and when Curtis got home and no one could tell him anything, well he went slap crazy in town. I had to give him something to calm him down so I could take him home. Now that I've had a chance to talk to you and I now know the truth, it's a bit easier to put the puzzle together. Okay enough of that, you need to get as much rest as you can and you must try to stay stress free. I'll tell Daniel the same thing and hopefully for the next month you'll get some peace. I'm afraid this also means you don't need to deal with your family right now. I'll come see you every week and we can talk, maybe that will help you deal with everything for now. Only one more thing, will you please call me Jonathan."

I smiled and said; "Thank you so very much Jonathan, I will look forward to seeing you again."

"Okay then, I'll explain all this to Daniel and I'll see you soon. Jonathan walked out of the bedroom and shut the door. Daniel must have been standing in the hall; I could hear Jonathan talking to him. Jonathan explained to Daniel about me needing my rest and no stress. He also told him I was eight months not seven and we needed to start preparing for the baby. Daniel asked Jonathan about having the baby at home and Jonathan said no way. There could be difficulties especially since I have not been monitored at all during this pregnancy. I could tell by Daniels voice he was not happy with that decision. I was so tired and I pulled the covers over me and went to sleep.

"Good morning sleepy head whispered Daniel. It's time to wake up, we need to go into town and go shopping for the baby."

"Oh okay. Give me a minute to take a shower and get dressed."

"Well hurry up. Here I brought you some juice. I hope you know what baby items to get?"

I laughed and said: "We need everything, from furniture to diapers."

"Oh, alright, well I'll wait for you downstairs."

I can't believe that I am going to have a baby in about a month. I wonder if it's a girl or boy. I hope it's a boy for Daniel's sake. As I started down the stairs I heard Daniel talking, oh it's Ms. Amy. I guess she's trying to find her way back to Daniel. I wonder how she really feels knowing I am his wife instead of her and I am the one giving him a child. The closer I got to the bottom of the stairs the more I could hear what they were saying and the louder Daniel's voice became.

I heard Ms. Amy say; "Daniel what were you thinking? Did you not realize that Curtis would be asking a lot of questions?"

Daniels voice became loud as he responded to her; "Amy I don't have time for this right now! Angela will be down any minute and were going to town. In case you didn't notice she's going to have my baby and we have to get ready for it."

"I always thought I would be the one having your baby." Ms. Amy replied. "You told me you loved me and I always did everything you asked, didn't I?"

Daniel looked like he was trying to walk away from her as he spoke back; "You did what I told you because you knew it was in your best interest to do so."

I could see Ms. Amy following behind him saying; "I did it because I loved you and I thought you loved me."

Daniel was getting angry at this point and said; "Amy I shouldn't have to tell you this, you should know that you're nothing but a cheap whore! Now get out of my house."

"If I'm a whore it's because you made me that way."

Tears were flowing so fast and her voice started to crack. "You made me sleep with you and with all your clients. You made me who I am today so how dare you condemn me for it. And if I'm a betting person, I bet your plans will be the same for Angela once she is no longer what you need."

I looked around the corner where I could still see them and Daniel slapped her across the face and she fell to the floor. I wanted to run to her but I didn't dare. Daniel grabbed her by the arm and dragged her out the door. Once they were outside I couldn't see or hear what they were saying anymore.

I slowly walked into the living room as Daniel walked back into the house.

He had a shocked look on his face and said; "How long have you been down here?"

"I just walked in here and was looking for you. It's not like I can move around very fast you know."

"I know honey; you just take your time. I'd rather you go slowly than to have something happen to you or my baby."

"You mean our baby Daniel. This baby belongs to the both of us."

"Glad to see you are looking at it that way as well."

"What is that suppose to mean?"

"Let's just go, I don't like the way the sky is looking, I think the weather going to turn bad."

Daniel called and had his driver pull up to the front of the house. I was getting pretty excited and then it hit me; who will we see in town, what do they know and what will they all say? On the way to town Daniel was going through some papers he had in his briefcase. It looked like he was into something that was very important so I didn't bother him. We were getting closer to town now and I started to shake. Daniel reached over and took my hand and lightly squeezed it. He looked at me and then smiled and I smiled back. He reached over and kissed me and told me not to worry, everything was going to be alright. It's moments like these that make me feel like I do love him in some odd way.

CHAPTER SEVENTEEN

It felt so good to be able to shop for the baby. Daniel was letting me pick out most of the items. "Honey I want you to get whatever you want." Daniel said.

He actually surprised me; he hasn't tried to take over like he normally does. I was getting some very odd and ugly looks; I can see them whispering to each other. I'm sure the only reason nothing has been said directly to me is mostly due to Daniel not leaving my side. People know him well enough not to speak ugly to me in front of him. Just about everyone in this town appears to be scared of him and I wish I knew why.

Jonathan walked in and said; "Well hello you two, I'm glad to see you're out shopping."

"Why hello there doctor." Daniel replied.

"Yes hello Dr. Jonathan and how are you?"

"Fine, thank you. Looks like you're finding a lot?"

"I just wish I knew if I was shopping for a boy or girl. It would make it so much easier." I told him.

"Well since you're in town, I can help you out with that, if you really want to know?"

"Oh yes I do, thank you. Daniel wouldn't you like to know as well? I asked him with excitement."

"I guess so." Daniel said, with no excitement at all.

"Good you can ride over to the hospital with me and we'll have a look."

We got into Dr. Jonathan's car and rode to the hospital which wasn't really that far away. I was so nervous and so excited at the same time.

We were about to see the baby and are going to find out if it's a girl or boy. Daniel looks a bit nervous too, I'm not sure if it's because it's his first child or because he's going to find out the sex. We followed Dr. Jonathan to the third floor and all the way down the hallway.

"Here we are, come on inside." He said. We entered into a small room with several machines and a table.

"Angela I need you to lie on that table and pull your dress up over your belly and pull your panties down just below your belly. There's a sheet you can cover up with."

I did just as he said and boy was that table cold, even with the pad and sheet on top of it. Of course Daniel was trying to cover me faster then I could uncover. Dr. Jonathan walked over and told me this gel would be very cold and he was sorry for the discomfort. He then turned on this machine and started rolling this object over my belly and within a few seconds we could hear the baby's heart beat.

Dr. Jonathan started laughing and said; "There it is. Look Angela, the baby is sucking its thumb."

"Oh! Look at that, how exciting! Just look at that Daniel, that's our baby."

"Let me see if I can get the baby to move just a bit so I can see what it is."

Dr. Jonathan started pushing on my belly and the baby didn't like that all, it started kicking and swinging its arms. Daniel walked right up on the screen looking as if he was in a daze.

"There we go can you see that? You're going to have a boy." Dr. Jonathan said.

Daniel grabbed the doctor's arm and asked him if he was sure and the doctor said yes very sure. Daniel ran to my side and started kissing me and I even saw a tear fall from his eye.

"We're going to have a boy; you are going to give me a son. Do you know how happy you just made me? Do you know how much I really truly love you? No one will ever take you or my son from me, not ever. We have so much to do Angela. I promise you Angela, I will make you happy and I will love you always, no one will ever hurt or upset you or my son. I dare anyone to even try."

"Okay then." Jonathan said. "Angela would you like a picture?"

"Yes thank you."

"You're so very welcome. Just give me a minute here. Oh look at that how about pictures of him sucking his thumb?"

"No! I forbid him to do that! I won't have any son of mine with a picture showing him sucking his thumb; Hey doc can't you stop him from doing that?"

"No Daniel. And believe it or not, it's perfectly normal for any child to do this and continue it after birth. They normally quit on their own and you can't really forbid them in this stage or even once they're born."

I was shocked at the way Daniel was acting. So I spoke up to him as well. "Daniel stop it your scaring me, you can't possible be upset with this can you? If you're going to react this way now what are you going to do once he's born?"

"Angela I'm sorry. I just don't want people to think I have a sissy for a son. That's all."

"Daniel no one would ever think that and even if they did they wouldn't dare say it." I explained to him.

"Daniel, infants don't realize what they are doing. They have to learn and as a parent you will have to teach him. That's how he'll learn and if he starts out sucking his thumb that doesn't mean he's going to be a sissy. You need to be very patient and understanding parent. At this stage in the game you could break his will power and turn him into a sissy yourself if your not careful." Jonathan told him.

Daniel responded; "I guess you know what you're talking about doctor; I didn't mean to react that way. I am sorry. Please give Angela any picture she likes."

Once Dr. Jonathan printed a picture out, he told me to go ahead and get up. He drove us back to the store and reminded Daniel that I needed to stay stress free and needed plenty of rest.

Once we got back in the store Daniel and I were both grabbing things. It almost felt like we had bought out the store. When we left that place we ended up hitting several more stores and before we knew it we had the car loaded down. Daniel told the driver to take the items back to the house and to carry all the packages upstairs. The driver nodded and then asked Daniel where he should pick us up at. Daniel told him not to worry about it; he would call for another car.

"Daniel what are we going to do? We bought everything we are going to need for the baby."

"Well my love, how about we eat a late lunch and take in a movie?"

"That's sounds wonderful."

We went to the little country diner and had lunch. While we were eating Daniel called the rental company and had them bring us a car. After we ate we went on to the movies. It was so nice to do something for a change without having to worry or having to look over your shoulder wondering what's going to happen next.

I looked at Daniel and asked him; "Are you happy now knowing we are going to have a son?"

"Yes I am, and I will make you just as happy if only you will let me."

I smiled at Daniel and replied; "We are going to have a son together, I do want to be happy and I want him to be happy."

"Then please Angela, you need to open up to me and let Curtis go."

Daniel put his arm around me and kissed my forehead. He placed his finger under my chin and raised my head so he could kiss me on the lips. I didn't feel shame or fear; I didn't even shiver or feel like my skin was crawling. Maybe I was falling in love with him. Maybe I was already in love with him. I have to let my feelings for Curtis go. Daniel and I are about to have a son who will need both of his parents, together to love and raise him in a good and happy home. I must get Curtis out of my head and my heart; I must do this for my son if nothing else. I don't know how long Daniel has to live, so it's very important I give him and our son all my attention.

When the movie was over we got into the car and drove around so we could see the leaves changing. Daniel stopped at this old fashion hotel; it was covered in lights and had a waterfall flowing in the front. Daniel drove around to the back where there was another road that had lighted trees on both sides of the drive. There were trees, bushes and flowers everywhere. There was even an old looking saw mill at the top of the hill. Daniel drove past it and behind the mill was a big restaurant that looked like it belonged in another world. I never knew all this was out here. Daniel came to a stop and helped me out of the car and another man took the keys so he could park it.

"Come along with me Angela, you are about to dine on the finest foods which most people only dream about." Daniel said.

This place looked like a palace inside and it smelled so good. The baby started kicking like he knew he was fixing to be fed. They took us to a private room with candles burning and a fireplace glowing, it was so romantic. This was the kind of place that would make you feel like you were in love even if you weren't.

"I'll order for us both; I want you and the baby to enjoy everything."

Daniel ordered our food and then he asked me to excuse him for only a minute. The next thing I heard was this music playing. It was so soft and gentle. I was becoming so relaxed I was afraid I was going to fall asleep. Daniel walked back into the room and the waiters were right behind him with our food. That food would melt in your mouth; it was so good I could hardly catch my breath. I saw Daniel looking at me from time to time grinning. Once we finished our meal Daniel said he would bring me back after the baby was born so we could really have a romantic night together. I have to tell you I can't wait for that day to come. Daniel looked at me and he could tell I was tired.

"Come on honey, I need to get you home so you and the baby can rest. We'll put all the baby items together and set them up where you want it first thing in the morning. Is that alright with you?"

"Oh yes Daniel that is perfectly fine with me. All I want to do now is go to bed. Thank you for such a wonderful day and evening it really meant a lot to me."

I looked back one more time as we drove away. This place was so breathe taking I almost hated to leave. As we drove through the night I started getting sleepy so I laid my head back.

Daniel softly rubbing my arm woke me up saying; "Angela honey wake up were home."

I rose up and Daniel got out of the car to help me out. He told someone to drive the car to the side so it could be picked up in the morning. We went upstairs and when we reached the bedroom Daniel helped me undress and get into my night clothes. I started to shiver from the cold air so he hurried to get me into bed and pulled the covers over me. He went over to the fireplace and built a fire. As I watched him I could see the glow from the fire on his body, as he walked back over to me and he kissed me goodnight. I couldn't help myself as I reached for him. "Daniel I don't want you to go, will you stay with me? Please."

"Yes of course my love, if you really want me too."

"Yes, I do."

I reached up and pulled him towards me. I began kissing him like I have never done before. I could see the shock in his eyes when he looked at me. He pulled away and stood up so he could undress and as he was doing so the glow from the fire was all over him. You could see the tan of his skin, the strength from his muscles, the softness of his hair and the gentleness in his eyes. I never really noticed him like this before. I found myself wanting him and when he climbed into the bed I placed my hand on his face and I kissed him. We had the most gentle and sweetest love making ever. I enjoyed it and I know Daniel did too. We laid there talking about our son and what we wanted for him. There were a several things Daniel said that we both agreed on. It was amazing that we felt the same about so many things. He wanted me to tell him how I wanted to arrange the baby's room and he thought that was okay. Daniel said he wanted to get another crib so the baby could sleep in our room, at least until we felt safe enough for him to sleep in his room. Daniel also wanted me to think about hiring a live in nanny to sleep in a connecting room with the baby's. Daniel held me in his arms as we talked, we must have talked for hours or at least until the two of us fell asleep.

CHAPTER EIGHTEEN

I woke up to the baby kicking, it even woke Daniel up.

"What the heck was that?" Daniel said as he turned over.

I laughed and said; "That's our son."

Daniel raised the covers looking at my belly and said; "Boy he sure does know how to kick, don't he?"

He placed his hand on my stomach as he watched our son move and kick. The morning light from the window was very bright as it shined across the room. I thought about Curtis and how he kept his curtains closed. I have to stop doing this; I have to get him out of my head. I have to make things work with Daniel I have to think of our son; he will need both of his parents.

"Angela would you like some coffee or juice?"

"I would really like a cup of hot tea."

"Alright I'll go down and get it. Hey how about when I get back we work on the baby stuff okay?"

"That sounds good." I replied.

Daniel left and I got up wrapping my housecoat around me. I walked to the window, it was so beautiful outside. The view was breath taking from this side of the house. From here you could see the semi cleared woods where there was a lake. Oh my goodness, it just dawned on me, its October no wonder everything is beginning to change. I had lost touch with time, days and even which month it was. Thanksgiving will be here in three weeks then Christmas I have so much to do, not to mention my son will be coming soon. I have to talk to Daniel about all this. I wonder if he has even thought of the holidays being so close. I ran to the door and when I opened it, I found Daniel standing there getting ready to come in. He gave me this shocked look and said; "Angela what the heck are you doing?"

"Oh Daniel, do you realize what month this is?"

He stood there with a tray of drinks and fruit in his hands, looking at me as if I had lost my mind. "Daniel do you realize Thanksgiving will be here in three weeks then Christmas, we have so much to do."

"Calm down Angela, we have time I'll get you all the help you need to get ready."

He walked in the bedroom and placed the tray down on the table next to the window.

"Honey, come here and calm down, I'm sure that isn't good for our son. Now here, sit down and drink your tea so we can talk about what you want done."

"Daniel I am so excited I don't know where to begin. Do you know our son will be here to have Christmas with us?"

"First we need to get his room ready, and then we'll start getting the house ready for the holidays. You make your list of what you want done and what food you want cooked. I'll go to town and hire more help just for you. Okay?"

"No Daniel, the thing about holidays is being able to do it all yourself."

"Angela, you're no condition to do much of anything yourself. But, I'll tell you what we can do. How about you and I go into town and get everything you want for Thanksgiving?"

"Daniel I know you're getting behind on work already, I can't ask you to take more time out for me."

"I'll do anything for you and my son, so don't ever think otherwise. If for any reason I can't go then someone from the house will. The main thing is for you not to be left alone, just in case something was to happen."

I understood what he was saying so I replied; "Okay that will be fine."

"Angela you can still be involved with everything, I just don't want you doing it yourself. You have to think about the baby. You'll have plenty of help and you can tell them where you want to put things and how you want the food cooked. I'm assuming you want to have guests over for the holidays?"

"Yes I would. Is that alright?"

"That's fine with me as long as you don't over do it and make yourself too tired."

"Oh Daniel thank you, I love you and this will be the best holiday season you have ever seen!"

As we sat there having our morning tea and coffee Daniel made a few phone calls. He was making arrangements to bring in some more household help for me. I have so many ideas on how we can decorate and the way I want the dinner to be fixed. I can tell he's so worried about me and the baby; he's willing to do what ever it takes to make me happy and keep me safe, just like he said. You know, I don't think people have given him a chance. They haven't taken the time to get to know him like I do. He really does have a good and gentle side.

"Angela honey, you need to take a shower and get dressed. I'll get some help up here to the baby's room and once we finish that, you can get started on your holiday list."

I jumped up, kissed him and did just as he said without any hesitation. Just wait until everyone comes; I want them to see we are happy. Most of all Curtis needs to believe that I am happy. I want him to be happy and I don't want him to go down the same road as his dad. I don't think he really knows the real truth, and right now I don't think he needs to know. It would just make matters worse for everyone. I want them all to get along, be able to come here and enjoy themselves and spend time with my son. I want my son to know all of his family. What name will I give to him? I must talk to Daniel about that too. Oh, so much to do, so much to think about. After my shower I dressed and went to the baby's room. Daniel and the boys were putting the furniture together so I got a pencil and pad. I started writing some of my ideas down, they were coming into my head faster then I could write. All of a sudden I realized I was beginning to live my life for the very first time, all because of Daniel. I know we started off on the wrong side of things, but he was willing to do what ever it took to convince me how much he loved me and how much we belonged together. I was just being stubborn; I wouldn't open up and give him a chance. He was right about one thing; I was shaming myself and my family for loving Curtis in a way that was forbidden.

I heard Daniel call out; "Hey darling are you dressed?"

"Yes I am and have started writing things down on this pad."

"Okay that's great honey. If you got a minute I would like for you to come over to the baby's room. We need to know where you want the furniture to go."

I reached out and took Daniels hand this time as we walked together. He looked at me and grinned as he bent down and kissed me. It didn't take long to get the furniture where I wanted it and best of all, Daniel didn't disagree with any of it. It looked perfect; this is going to be the best baby room ever! I was feeling a little hungry; I looked at the clock, it was past twelve.

I pulled at Daniels arms and said; "It's after twelve and I'm hungry, we need to eat something." Daniel nodded and we headed downstairs into the kitchen. The cook had already prepared lunch for us; oh this is so nice having everything already done for you. It won't take me long to get used to this.

"Angela, after lunch I'm going into town to hire two more people for the house. They'll be here to work for you only. Any outside work you want done just let me know; I'll get some of the outside hands to do that. Okay?"

"Okay Daniel and thank you."

"I'm your husband and you are about to be the mother of my son. Haven't you realized by now that it's my job to take care of everything so you don't have to worry? I love you sweetheart, I have always loved you."

"I can see that now and I'm so sorry I fought you for so long, can you ever forgive me?"

"Baby there is nothing to forgive. Now while I'm out, I want you to continue working on your list. Just as soon as I return, we'll get started on it."

"Daniel how long will you be gone?"

"I'm afraid I'll be gone for a while. I have to do these interviews and I also have some work I need to get caught up on. Honey don't you worry none, I'll be back in time for dinner."

Daniel got up from the table and kissed me goodbye. I went right back to work on my list, before I knew it I had written over four pages. There were so many things I wanted to do and people I wanted to invite. I was getting tired and Daniel wouldn't be home for several hours, so I went upstairs to lie down. Between getting the baby's room ready and the excitement of being able to set up for the holidays I had over exerted myself.

CHAPTER NINETEEN

I woke up to someone calling out my name and when I opened my eyes it was Curtis. I panicked and whispered; "Curtis what are you doing here? Does Daniel know you're here?"

"No Angela, no one saw me. I need to talk to you. I need to know the real truth and I want to hear it from you."

"What truth?"

"Angela I need to know the real truth about you and Daniel? The truth about what part my father played in it? The truth about how you still feel about me?"

"I don't know what to really say to you. You know I'm going to have Daniel's baby."

"Josh has tried to tell me, but he's been doing it in bits and pieces. I want to know everything and you're the only person who can do that. Please Angela will you just tell me?"

"Okay Curtis, but your not going to like what you hear and you may not even believe it."

"Please, I need to know what happened after I left."

I sat up hanging my legs off the side of the bed. Curtis stood in front of me as I began telling him everything about his father, the drinking, and the bedroom. I told him how Brad was thinking I was my mother Mary. I told him about the bills; how Daniel got in the picture and how I got the way I am now. As I was telling him, I could see his anger overwhelming him and he fell to his knees. As hard as it was I continued, he laid his head in my lap and cried. I didn't want to continue anymore but I knew I had to. Curtis wasn't the type of person to let something go and he always was one who had to have all the facts. He cried like I had never seen before, not even when my mom died.

"Angela I am so sorry baby. I am so sorry that my father did that to you. Be honest with me, are you truly happy now? Do you really love Daniel?"

I looked Curtis directly into his eyes and said; "I'm not sure what I feel. He's been so good to me since we've been back and I guess I do feel like I am falling in love with him. But none of that really matters anymore. I am about to give birth to Daniels son and I will not let this child suffer for the mistakes that were made. He will have both of his parents raising him and I hope in a loving and caring home. Curtis you have to leave, if Daniel finds out that you're here he'll go crazy."

With tears still in his eyes Curtis asked; "Be honest and tell me one more thing, do you still love me?"

I couldn't lie to him so I said; "Yes, I still love you, I will always love you. I will never love a man the way I love you, but what we had wasn't right. Even you knew that and tried to stop it. I was the one who didn't help matters. I continued to go to you even after you told me to stop, so I take full blame for everything."

"No my love, we are both at fault and being older, I should have taken more control of myself. I'm still your brother and I refuse to be taken out of your life or out of your baby's life. I think it's only fair that I have the right to be in it."

"I do agree with you and I will talk to Daniel. I'm not sure how he will feel, but I think I can get him to understand."

"So, you and Daniel are going to have a son? I have to tell you Angela that does make me jealous, but at the same time I am happy for you."

"Curtis, let's go down stairs and get something to drink." Curtis helped me up and we went downstairs to the kitchen. I was pouring us some hot tea when Daniel walked in with the most unapproved look. I knew I had better respond to him quickly; "Daniel I'm glad your home, I guess it didn't take you as long as you thought. Look Curtis is here to give us his blessings."

"Is that right?" Daniel said as he stared directly at Curtis.

"Yes Daniel that's right. You've got a good lady here and I assure you I'm only here as her brother, and your brother-in-law, to wish you both happiness and congratulations."

"That's very nice of you Curtis. May I speak with you outside?"

Daniel and Curtis both walked out of the kitchen door, my heart felt like it stopped beating. I was so scared for both of them.

"Curtis, why are you really here?" Daniel asked.

"I told you Daniel, I wanted to give you my blessing."

"No Curtis, I think there was more to it. You see I figured out the secret you and Angela had."

"Okay Daniel. You want me to be honest with you, okay here goes. I needed to hear the truth from Angela about what happened when I left. I have to say; what you and my father did to her was dead wrong and I will be confronting my father when I get back to the house."

"Curtis I agree with that. How we went about it was wrong, but I love your sister. I also knew if I didn't take control of the situation with your father, there's no telling who would have gotten Angela. So you see, the way I see it, she was lucky I was the one who stepped in. She could have been passed around to any man who would give money to your father. His drinking had gotten that bad, so I did what I had to do to save her and your family. Curtis, your father and I have been friends for many years and I knew the drinking was making him do the things he did. The man lost both of his wives, he was losing you and then knowing he was about to lose everything else including Angela. I couldn't let that happen and at the same time I had to save Angela. After all, you left them and there was no one else she could turn to, she needed someone to help her!"

"I guess I need to thank you Daniel. I had no idea it had gotten so bad. I'll deal with my father don't you worry about that. He'll have to look in that mirror and face what he has done to everyone. Tell me this, how did you find out about me and Angela?"

"I don't think that matters now, do you? Look Curtis, I don't need any problems here. As you can see she's happy now and I can give her anything she wants or needs. Basically I'm asking you to walk away, don't take her back into that shame you were living in before."

"Daniel, I don't know what you said to Angela when you found out about me and her, but we were not living in shame. We loved one another and were not related by blood and I have no intentions of walking away. But I will give you my word that I will only see her as my sister and nothing more. Your son will be my nephew; I would like to take him fishing, and hunting. When he's older I would like to take him riding on the tractor around the farm. You have nothing to fear from me Daniel unless you hurt her. If you would accept it I would like to offer you my friendship."

"Thank you Curtis I would like that. Angela is getting pretty excited about the holidays and having family and friends over would mean a great deal to her."

"If that's an invitation, then I accept. I would love to come and I'm sure dad and Josh would too."

"Good. I'm glad we were able to get all this behind us and able to move on so we can be a family. What do you say we go back inside now before Angela has that baby?"

Daniel and Curtis were laughing as they came back in the door. I can't tell you what a relief that was. We sat around the table drinking hot tea, talking and laughing. The cook finally ran us out so she could cook dinner.

"Curtis, would you like to stay and have dinner with Angela and me?" Daniel asked.

"Thanks Daniel maybe some other time. I really need to get back to the farm."

Curtis got up, kissed me on my forehead and started walking towards the living room door. Daniel reached out his hand to Curtis and said; "If you need any help just let me know."

"Thanks Daniel. Angela I'm glad we finally got to talk. I'm sorry I left home, but I'm very happy for you and Daniel. I'll see you both real soon and Daniel I don't want you to be a stranger at the farm."

"Thanks I'll see you over their sometime. You take care now and don't be too hard on your dad, you hear me?"

"Yea Daniel, I hear you. I want to thank both of you for being so open and honest with me."

I watched Curtis walk out the door. I reached over to Daniel and hugged him as tight as I could. He looked at me funny and hugged me back as if to say, it's okay. Then he said; "Angela your new help will be here first thing Monday morning. I figured that way it would give you a couple days to really think of what you want done."

I looked into his eyes and with a smile I said; "Thank you Daniel for everything."

"Angela you don't have to keep doing that, I told you I am here to take care of you and to protect you. I love you and I have always loved you that will never change. What do you say about us sitting by the fireplace watching a little TV before dinner?"

"Daniel, I think that is a very good idea."

CHAPTER TWENTY

The baby kicked and moved all night long. I didn't sleep very well and I knew it had disturbed Daniel too. Well he looks like he's sleeping okay now, so I grabbed my robe and went on downstairs. Daniel allowed everyone Sundays off which was fine with me. It was pretty nice to have an empty house for a change. I went into the kitchen to start some breakfast and put some coffee on. I haven't done any cooking since we've been back, although I do have to say it's been nice, though I do like to cook. I was raised to cook, clean and take care of everyone and that's pretty hard to just shut off.

I heard Daniel coming down the stairs calling out to me; "Angela, honey what are you doing?"

"I wasn't sleeping very well so I decided to cook some breakfast, besides I haven't been able to cook for you since we came home."

"That's very sweet of you. I want you to know that I've noticed how you have been trying to show me you love me and I want to thank you for that."

I smiled and replied; "That's my job as your wife and the mother of your son."

Daniel laughed and said; "Okay good one! I'm going to get the newspaper off the porch. Call me when you have breakfast ready."

After breakfast, Daniel and I went over my list and he thought everything looked okay, and said my help will be here first thing in the morning. Daniel decided to go into town so we could do some shopping. We shopped in almost every store and bought a lot of things. We stopped at the café for lunch before we drove outside of town to shop at some more stores and we ate dinner out too. It was so late by the time we got home I just wanted to go to bed. Daniel stayed up because he said he had some papers to go through.

The next morning I realized he hadn't been to bed so I went downstairs to see if I could find him. I found him asleep in his office chair so I very carefully woke him up. I wanted to make sure he was okay. He said he was fine but didn't have time for coffee or breakfast. He said he had to hurry into town; he had several meetings lined up for today. He ran upstairs to shower and change so I grabbed a cup of coffee and sat it on the bathroom counter. I sat on the edge of the bed and waited for him. When he saw the coffee he came out and kissed me.

"Thank you Angela, this was very sweet of you." He smiled, got dressed and handed me the empty cup. As he kissed me good-bye he said; "I'll see you later tonight. Do not over do it today or I will be very upset with you!"

Before I could respond he turned and walked out the door. I followed him downstairs and to the front door. As he was walking out, the people he hired were standing on the front porch. Dr. Jonathan was standing behind them smiling.

I smiled and said; "Good morning everyone I am so glad you're here. We went to town yesterday and bought everything that we needed to get started. You will find some of the items are here already and the rest will be delivered sometime this morning. If you would, please keep an eye out for the driver and help him get everything unloaded. You can put what he brings inside the storage room which is right over there under the stairs. You will find some bags already in the storage area so if you want, you can go ahead and get started on unpacking those things. There's plenty of shelves so you can separate and organize it all. I'll be with the good doctor here and I will be back down to guide everyone through the rest. You can see the cook for drinks or food when ever you're ready for that as well."

I turned facing Jonathan and replied; "Well Doctor, shall we go upstairs?"

"Lead the way Mrs. Moore."

"Please call me Angela not Mrs. Moore."

"Mrs. Moore will do in front of your help, Angela will do elsewhere. Your husband insists on it and we don't want to upset him, now do we?"

"Okay I can see that coming from him, he's so protective of me."

"A little too much if you ask me."

"Why do you say that?"

"I'm sorry I guess I should just keep my mouth shut."

"No, what do you mean?"

"We'll talk later when you come to my office. Right now let's get you checked out and see how that baby is doing."

My check up went well and the baby's been dropping so Jonathan told me I needed to be more careful. I showed the doctor out and went to the storage area so we could get started putting things up. It went by quicker then I thought even though it took us all day and everything looks good. I talked with the cook about the Thanksgiving menu and we went over the guest list along with my other helpers. Daniel still wasn't home yet, but he did say he would be late. I was so tired after dinner and went on to bed. Early the next morning Daniel woke me up to tell me how nice everything looked but he had to leave on the jet and wouldn't be back until the next day. I didn't want him to go but he had too. Later that day I started feeling sick and the baby was being so active that I decided to lie down. I stayed in bed for the rest of that day. The cook sent food up to my room but I just couldn't eat it. Later that night I got up to work on the invitations for the Thanksgiving dinner party; after all, we only had a little over a week to go. Once I finished I took them to the mailbox, then went back to bed.

Daniel woke me up when he came in and said he heard I wasn't feeling well and I wasn't eating. He was a little upset and said I needed to think of the baby and eat something. He had the cook send up a tray of food and juice and told me to sit up and eat or there would be no Thanksgiving party. For a moment there, I felt like I was a two year old child and being fussed at by my father, but I knew it's only because he's worried about me. I ate what I could and then I got dressed and went downstairs. Daniel was in his study and I knew not to disturb him when he had the door closed. I went to the living room to wait for him. I was looking at the newspaper but wasn't really reading it. I wanted to talk to Daniel about the dinner party. When he finally came out he didn't have time to talk, he had to go to town. I asked if I could go and he said no, that I needed to stay close to home and he would see me later. He kissed me bye and walked out.

The day went by very slowly and I couldn't rest, I was getting restless and lonely. I would like to see Curtis and Josh; I decided to go to the farm. I asked Sherry who was one of my helpers to come join me and I asked Juan who was my other helper to bring one of the cars around and drive me over to my family's farm. Within minutes he had the car in front and we left. I hadn't been out to the farm for almost two years. Before we got there I started getting this awful pain and I felt like I was going to throw up. Juan stopped the car and ask if he should take me home or to the hospital. I told him to take me to Dr. Jonathan's office. Dr. Jonathan checked me out and everything was fine but he told me to go home, slow down and get some rest. I went home got into bed and Maria the cook came up to check on me. She told me not worry about a thing, they will handle everything for me and I just needed to rest. She later brought me something to drink and eat and said if I didn't at least try Mr. Moore will become very angry. I told her not to worry, it will be alright and I would try. Shortly after I drank my milk I fell asleep.

When I woke up it was morning, I guess I had slept the rest of the day and night away. I got up looking for Daniel but he was in his study with the door closed again. I went back upstairs to shower and change. Sherry told Maria I was up so Maria cooked me some breakfast and had Sherry bring it up to my room.

"Mrs. Angela I brought you some breakfast." Sherry said quietly.

"Thank you Sherry, just put the tray on the stand by my chair, I'll be out shortly."

I stepped out of the bathroom went to eat my breakfast. Daniel walked in and he looked very angry. "Daniel what's wrong?" I asked him.

"What's wrong? You have the nerve to ask me what's wrong. I told you to stay close to home and what do you do; you decide to go for a joy ride. You decided to go for a drive to your family's farm. You put my son's life in danger and I will not stand for that. Do you under stand me?"

"Daniel, don't you think you're over reacting just a bit?"

"If you want to see over reacting then just try leaving this house again without my approval."

"What! So you're going to keep me here like a prisoner?"

"I will do what I have to for the safety of my son and any court will agree with me."

"Okay Daniel now you're scaring me, I think you are really over reacting right now. I just got a little sick and I was checked out by the doctor and everything is fine."

"Like I said Angela, you will not leave here again without my approval. I have given strict orders to all the help not to take you anywhere unless I give the okay."

Daniel walked out and slammed the door my heart was beating so fast it felt like it was going to jump out of my chest. He is starting to change and I can't understand why. I thought things were going so good between us; until he got back involved in his work. I still don't know what it is he does, I need to get into that office and see what's going on. I'll have to find a way the next time he's out. He kept himself closed up in his office most of the day and had the cook bring him a tray of food. I waited for him in the living room but he never stepped out of that room. I finally went back to my room and went on to bed.

CHAPTER TWENTY-ONE

The next morning I woke up to Daniel climbing into bed.

"Good morning Daniel, happy Thanks-giving."

"Good morning Angela, how are you feeling today?"

"I'm feeling fine, why do you ask?"

"Maybe I'm asking because I care, is that alright with you?"

After saying that; Daniel jumped up out of bed and went into the bathroom slamming the door. He's getting really good about slamming doors and walking away. I walked to the bathroom door.

"Daniel what's going on with you? You are getting so snappy and you don't spend anytime at home or with me anymore, what's going on with you? Is there anything I can do to help?"

I heard the shower cut on and I tried to open the door but he had locked it. Something is going on but what? I hope he gets his act together before our guests arrive for dinner. I sat in my chair and waited for him to come out.

When the door opened I jumped up and headed right for him. "Please Daniel will you just talk to me? What is going on with you?"

"Angela I don't need this from you right now. I've got a lot on my plate and you are only making it worst by trying to take off. I even asked you to stay close to home. You could have harmed my son as well as yourself, or don't you care? Haven't I been doing everything you asked of me? Why can't you give me the same respect? That's all I ask, just give me some respect."

"I'm so sorry Daniel. I didn't mean to make things hard on you, please forgive me. I'll stay here and won't go anywhere without talking to you first, okay?"

"Can you really promise me that and keep it?"

"Daniel Honey, I promise, I do love you. Please don't be angry with me. I want you to have a good time tonight at our dinner party."

"So that's it? This is all about your damn dinner party?"

"No, I swear it isn't. I just didn't like you staying gone and not talking to me. Please Daniel don't be like this please."

Before Daniel could respond back I felt this horrible pain and had to reach for something before I fell. Daniel's eyes widened as he ran to catch me.

"Angela, are you alright?"

"Please help me to the chair I need to sit down."

Daniel picked me up and carried me to the bed and laid me down. Then he ran to the phone and called Dr. Jonathan to come over right away.

"Angela I am so sorry. I shouldn't have acted that way towards you."

"It's okay Daniel, I'm sure everything is fine."

Daniel opened the door and told Jose to watch out for the doctor and to have the cook bring Angela a cup of hot tea. I reached out my hand to Daniel and said; "Please come here, I need for us to talk. I don't want you angry at me, our baby is due anytime and we have guest and family coming for dinner tonight."

"Angela I'm not angry, just scared. As long as you keep your promise not to leave this house without me knowing where you are going, and that includes after our son is born."

"Alright fine, I promise."

"Did you really mean what you said about loving me?"

"Yes, I do."

Before anything else could be said Jose was knocking on the door.

"The doctor is here" he cried out.

Daniel opened the door to let the Dr. in and he asked Daniel to step out while he checked me. "Angela what's going on with you?"

"Just a lot of sleepless nights, sometimes I can't eat and I am having a lot of hard pains." I replied.

"Well that's to be expected; the baby could come at anytime now. Let me get Daniel in here." As Daniel walked in, Jonathan said he needed to talk to the both of us. "Angela can go into labor at anytime so I suggest she doesn't go off rambling, no stress of any kind, get plenty of fluids and most of all get plenty of rest. Make sure someone is here with her at all times."

"I'll make sure of it Doc. Well it's four o'clock and the dinner party starts at six so why don't you go ahead and stay? There's really no reason to run home is there?"

"I'd love to but I have another house to go to. After that I'll stop by my house for a shower and I'll come back by here a little later. Angela take care of yourself and I do believe your little bundle of joy will be here really soon. I'll show myself out Daniel, you just make sure she stays here and rests until it's time for her to show up for the party."

"Will do and thanks doctor, I'll see you at six. Angela you stay here and rest, I'll make sure everything is just the way you want it. I'll come up to help you get ready later okay?"

"Okay. I am tired; I think I'll just take a quick nap."

"That's my girl. I'll be back up in a little bit."

Daniel walked out and I was relieved to see him acting so much better and hopefully he'll stay that way through dinner. At least I pray that he does.

CHAPTER TWENTY-TWO

Daniel woke me up telling me it's time to get ready. I could smell the food and it smelled so good. I am so excited; all of my family and friends are going to be here. I hope everything goes well. I got dressed and started down the stairs where I saw Curtis and Josh talking, and then I saw Brad and Ms. Amy. It looks like they may be together now. Oh there's Dr. Jonathan, he did make it back! There are even some people here I don't know; I guess Daniel invited them. He must have forgotten to tell me he's been so busy.

Josh walked up to me and said; "Angela you look so lovely."

"Well thank-you so much Josh."

"Yes." Brad said. "I must say you look more and more like your mother everyday."

"Thank-you Brad, that means a lot to me."

Curtis stepped in front of Brad and said; "You look so beautiful. I think being pregnant made you even more beautiful, which I didn't think possible."

"Thank-you Curtis, you are too kind."

"Yes, well Angela would you like something to drink?" Daniel asked.

I'm sure it was also to stop that conversation.

"Yes Daniel thank-you."

"Hello Jonathan I'm glad to see you were able to make it back in time. Hello Ms. Amy how are you two doing?"

"Angela I want to thank-you for inviting me." Ms. Amy responded.

"I have no hard feelings towards you Ms. Amy. I'm glad you were able to come."

"That's my girl." Daniel said as he handed me a glass of punch. "You see she's so happy with me that she has no time to worry about you or the past. Isn't that right sweetheart?"

"Yes dear, that's right. I have to think about my baby now."

"Speaking of baby, I hear you could be having that little one at anytime." Curtis replied.

"Yes, that's right Curtis" said Daniel, "We could have our son at any time so please, I must ask you all not to say or do anything that could stress Angela out."

Curtis looked a little disgusted and said; "Daniel I think we all know not to cause a fuss. As her brother, I made that remark because we are all excited as well!"

I could see the blood vessel popping up in Daniel's head. He doesn't take it well when people correct him or question anything he may have said.

There were so many people here I don't know and Daniel never introduced me to any of them. "Daniel would you like to introduce me to your guests?" I asked him.

"In a bit honey, I have something I need to check on."

As he walked out of the room I noticed a very nice looking lady with very long legs, slender built and fire red hair. I noticed her because she seemed to want to stay very close to Daniel. The cook stepped in and told everyone that dinner's on the table. I was looking for Daniel so we could walk in together but he was no where to be found. Jonathan took my arm and as we walked into the dinning area he asked me if I was alright. I was fine I told him.

The table was set-up so beautiful, a little different then what I had wanted but it still looked very nice. Then I noticed the flowers were not the ones I asked for, nor was that the menu the one I had written. What is going on here? This is not what I had requested. I mustn't show any signs of disappointment, it may get Daniel upset. We all sat down and the red headed lady sat by Daniel at the other end of the table. Every few minutes she would reach for his hand and hold it. They did a lot of touching and laughing as if no one else was in the room. By the time we had reached the middle of the meal I couldn't stand it anymore.

"Please excuse me I will be right back."

"Darling are you alright?" Daniel asked.

"Yes Daniel I need to be excused just for a minute."

"What's wrong, do you need to lie down?"

"No Daniel, I have to relieve myself if you really need to know."

After I said that I walked away from the table. I knew Daniel did not like the way I responded back to him. I walked into the kitchen to talk to the cook when Daniel walked in and grabbed my arm. He slung me around so hard I almost lost my balance.

"What kind of remark was that?"

"Daniel I was trying to be discreet and you kept questioning me and I had no other way to put it where you would understand. And by the way, what happened to the menu? What happened to the flowers I asked for? Nothing out there is what I had requested."

"Melissa came over to help get everything set up. You needed your rest and I had my hands full."

"Who's Melissa?"

"Oh, I haven't introduced you. She's my assistant; I hired her before we left to get married. She's been running things for me while we were away. She's really very good."

"Yes, I bet she is. So why did she change what I had requested?"

"Oh stop it, you're behaving like a child. She has done us a favor. So you actually owe her a thank you and I do expect you to give her one."

"I will not, she changed everything! She made this her dinner party instead of mine."

"You stop that, your hear me? I will not have you acting like a child and you will do what I say. I asked her to come here and help. She didn't hesitate one minute, she came right over. So you should be grateful to her. Now let's go back to our guests and you better behave yourself."

We went back to the table where she was laughing and talking to everyone as if she were the hostess. The worst thing is everyone was responding to her. This was no longer my party it was hers and it looks like she has Daniel too. I sat down and gave everyone time to complete their meal.

"Hello everyone, if you are all finished you will find drinks in the other room."

Melissa looked at me and said; "Yes let's do that, and Daniel you really need to tell our guests your story?"

What! I thought. She said our guest, speaking of her and Daniel. Who does she think she is?

Daniel looked at her and grinned; "What story are you talking about Melissa?"

"You know when we went out of town for that meeting and how we got all the dates wrong and so we decided to go see an old friend of yours."

So these meetings he had to go on, it was with her. He's been lying to me all this time.

"Oh yes, now I know what you're talking about. That did turn out pretty funny didn't it?"

As Daniel and Melissa started laughing I could see they had everyone's attention. I was becoming so angry that I could feel my blood boil. I started to wonder how long he's been sleeping with her, why didn't he use her to have his child! I was so wrapped up with the two of them I didn't notice Curtis standing beside me.

"Angela you don't look so good, are you okay?"

"Yes Curtis thank you, I'm fine."

"No your not, its Melissa isn't it?"

"How could you know?"

"I'm a man."

"What is that suppose to mean?"

"I can see how she looks at Daniel and the way he looks back at her. Most of all, they can't seem to keep their hands off each other."

"So I'm not crazy?"

"No honey your not. Is there anything I can do?"

I started to cry and I reached for Curtis. He put his arms around me telling me everything will be okay.

"Curtis I don't know what I'm going to do. Even if Daniel is sleeping with that woman he will never let me leave and even if by some miracle he does, he will never let our son go."

"Don't worry little one I'm here. I'll help you no matter what you decide."

"Curtis let go of my wife!" Daniel yelled as he jumped on Curtis like a wild cat hitting me in the process, causing me to fall over the dining room chair which has two points on each side that pushed into my stomach. It took my breath away. Everyone else came running into the room and Dr. Jonathan ran over to me to see if I was okay. Only I couldn't move.

Jonathan yelled; "Daniel and Curtis you men need to stop fighting. We need to get Angela to the hospital."

They both looked at me with this crazed look in their eyes, and then I heard everyone talking about all the blood that was flowing from my body. It felt like people were grabbing at me from all angles and every touch made my body burn. Dr. Jonathan called for an ambulance and told everyone to move away from me. The next thing I knew I was going into labor but I was losing so much blood that everything was going dark and then it went completely black from me going unconscious.

CHAPTER TWENTY-THREE

I woke up in a very strange room; I had no idea where I was. I felt like I had been through hell and back. I felt so stiff and I had all these machines hooked to me. I started to panic when I heard this voice.

"Oh my goodness; are you waking up Mrs. Moore?"

I turned my head to see this woman all dressed in white. I tried to talk but it was a bit ruff. She gave me a drink of water and then I was able to say; "Who are you?"

"I'm Maggie your nurse. Your husband Mr. Moore hired me to take care of you."

"Why, where am I and how long have I been here?"

"This is a private hospital and after spending over a year in the local hospital, Mr. Moore decided to move you over here. I guess that was about six months ago. He was hoping if you were here you would be able to recover."

"Recover from what?"

"You don't remember anything?"

"No not really."

"You just lay still and I'll get Dr. Jonathan."

I was so thirsty and tried to sit up to see if I could grab that water but I couldn't get my body to rise up. Where exactly am I?

"I can't believe it! Hello Angela!" said Jonathan as he walked into the room.

"Hello, may I please have some more water?" I said and still unsure of where I was. "What has happened to me and why am I here?"

"Do you remember anything?" Jonathan replied.

"Not really. Why does everyone keep asking me that? Why won't anyone tell me why I'm here?"

"Well, you were having you're Thanksgiving dinner party and after dinner we all left the room. Daniel started telling us a story about his trip. Brad asked where you were so Daniel went back to find you. The next thing we knew, Daniel and Curtis were fighting and you were on the floor lying in a pile of blood. You passed out and I called the ambulance to have you taken to the hospital. You went into labor and I had to take the baby by c-section at which time I had to call for another doctor because you had to have major surgery. It didn't look good for you for awhile. You had internal bleeding and; oh Angela I am so sorry; so many things went wrong for you that night and you fell into a coma. You've been in a coma for over a year and a half."

"Where's my son? Is he okay"

"Daniel has your son and he's a fine boy. Angela I need you to stay calm, I have more to tell you."

"I want to see my son."

"Alright I'll call him, but first Angela I must tell you the rest."

"What is it Jonathan?"

"You can't have anymore children."

"What?"

"I'm sorry, but there was a lot of damage and the doctor did what he could to save you.

"What else happened?"

"I'm sorry to have to tell you this but Curtis is gone."

"Why, where did he go?"

"He was so upset over what had happened that he knocked Daniel out cold. On his way out the door he stopped and had words with his dad and knocked him out too. He jumped in your jeep and was going to follow the ambulance to the hospital. Josh ran after him begging Curtis to let him drive. Josh told Curtis he was to upset to drive himself. Curtis told Josh to keep Daniel and Brad away from the hospital or he would kill them both and he took off. Josh went back inside the house and heard Melissa on the phone; she had called the police telling them Curtis had started a fight and threatened to kill Daniel. Josh tried to stop her but it was too late. He called the police back to tell them she was mistaken only they had already sent out several patrol cars. We were told they were following behind him trying to get him to stop.

"No. No you're lying to me."

"I'm so sorry, I wish I were."

Crying I asked him; "Do you really believe them?"

"No. We found out later that they put up a road block just miles from the hospital. Curtis tried to go around it but one of the officers shot out two of his tires causing him to lose control of the jeep. He hit a tree and the jeep flipped several times throwing Curtis. His head hit a very large rock and that killed him instantly."

"You know Daniel has them on his payroll and I can proof it."

I started losing it. I began to cry uncontrollably screaming as loud as I could. Dr. Jonathan had the nurse give me a sedative shot through the IV. I tried to fight them but I was too weak and I drifted off to sleep. In my dreams it all came back to me. Everything came back to me. And when I woke back up the room was filled with flowers. Brad was asleep in a chair beside my bed. I reached out to touch his hand and he jumped. He sat there staring at me as if I were a ghost.

"Hello Brad, Dr. Jonathan told me about Curtis and I am so sorry."

"We buried him between his two mothers. Oh my sweet little one, I am so sorry! I blame myself for everything that has happened to you and to my son. I know in my heart he was taken away from me because of what I did to you. Please forgive me Angela. I didn't know what I was doing at the time. I know blaming the booze doesn't make it right, but truly I did things while I was drinking that I normally would not have done."

"I'm sorry too. I want you to get out of my room now"

"Please Angela, Please don't do this to me, please."

"I need time to deal with his death and what has happened to me. I can't deal with you too right now. Maybe I can later, but not right now."

"Alright, I understand. I know you have a lot to deal with and I'm asking you to forgive me for a lot of things. I'll be at the farm waiting to hear from you when ever you're ready to see me. You may not believe me but I do love you."

Josh walked into the room as Brad was walking out. Tears were forming in his eyes. I reached my hand out to him and as he took it he said; "I'm so sorry Angela, I tried to stop him."

"So I was told. It's okay Josh; I don't blame you for anything. I didn't just go to sleep this last time did I?"

"No you didn't"

"How long was I out this time?"

"Close to six months."

"What? You have to be joking!"

"No I'm not. Jonathan called me right after they gave you that sedative."

"Is Daniel and my son here?"

"No honey they're not, but Daniel did send most of the flowers."

"Will you please call him and ask him to bring my son. I want to see my baby."

"I'll call him, but first I need to let Jonathan know you're awake again."

Three nurse's came in and then Dr. Jonathan. I felt like a pin cushion the way everyone was picking and poking at me.

"Angela you will have to go through a lot of rehab before you can go home. You will need to build your muscles back up so you can walk and you need to start eating on your own. It will make you a bit sick at first but you're a strong woman and I have a lot of faith in you. Once you are able to go home you will still have to do rehab daily."

Josh walked back into the room and said, "I called Daniel and he will be here shortly to see you."

"Is he going to bring my son?"

"I don't think so. I think he wants to see you alone first. Look sweetie I need to get back to the farm is there anything else you want me to do?"

"No thank you Josh. Will you come back to see me?"

"You know I will. Love you little one." Josh and I both had a lot of pain and hurt inside us. I know I can help him but not until I can get better and get out of here.

"Dr. Jonathan, I just want you to know that I remember everything. I hope if I come to you for answers to fill in the blanks you will be honest with me."

"Angela I will tell you anything you want to know, that is as long as I know the correct answer."

"Thank you. Jonathan. I can't tell you how much it means to me to have a true friend."

"I am your friend. I'll stand by you and I will help you through it all. I have to go now I have to make rounds at the hospital but I'll be back just as soon as I can."

"Thank you. I'll be here waiting for you."

Jonathan laughed and said; "Glad to see you still have you're sense of humor."

CHAPTER TWENTY-FOUR

The nurses rushed Jonathan out so they could give me a bath and change my clothes. They brought me a plate of soft foods and a lot of liquids. It wasn't easy getting some of that down but they said I did well enough. I was determined to do what I had to so I could go home. I couldn't believe how tired I was after sleeping for two years, but the nurse told me that was normal. It didn't take long before I fell asleep. I woke up to Daniel calling my name and when I opened my eyes there he stood. He sat on the side of the bed pulling me upwards so he could hug me. "Angela honey, I am so glad you came out of that coma."

"Where's my son Daniel?"

"I didn't bring him, we needed time to see each other first and talk. I need time to explain who you are to him."

"What do you mean? He doesn't know me? You didn't bring him here to see me so he would know who his mother is?"

"I did at first, but he didn't understand."

"So you just decided to keep him away?"

"I did what I thought was best for him at the time. Honey I didn't know what all to do! Thank heaven for Melissa; once again she stepped up to the plate."

"Melissa has been taking care of my son? You let the woman who killed Curtis raise my son?"

"It wasn't her fault Curtis died. She's been helping me. He needed a mother, he was only a baby, and what else was I suppose to do?"

"Melissa has been playing the roll of his mother? How could you do that to me? Is she living in the house and playing the roll of your wife as well?"

"I did what I had to do. Danny needed a mother and she offered to help me and I accepted."

"Of course she did. Is Danny the name you gave him?"

"I named him Daniel Jr. and we call him Danny. After all you were in a coma and I had a son to take care of. So don't you dare judge me for doing what I had to do! You know with this attitude I don't think it would be in Danny's best interest to bring him here."

Daniel got up and walked out the door.

I began screaming as loud as I could; "Daniel don't you walk away from me! Daniel I want to see my son. Daniel, please come back, I want to see my baby."

I went to chase him but instead I fell out of bed. I had no strength in my legs; it was as if I were paralyzed. The nurses came running and helped me back in the bed. They told me to calm down or they would have to give me a sedative. I didn't want them to do that, it might put me back into another coma or at the very least a long sleep.

I realized I had to get better really fast. I knew I was going to have a big fight on my hands and could lose my son forever. One of the nurses called Jonathan and he came running into my room.

"Angela I heard what happened, are you okay?"

"Yes, thank you Jonathan. I need for you to be honest, how long will my recovery take?"

"It could take a long time. It's been two years and your body went through quite a trauma, not to mention the coma."

"I need to recover and I need to do it quickly! You know as well as I do I could lose Danny. Daniel already has him believing Melissa is his mother!"

"Yes I know. She moved into the house the same day Daniel took Danny home. She brought Danny to my office and she documented everything as his mother. When I refused to accept her doing that, Daniel had her take him to another doctor out of town."

"Well at least I'm on the birth certificate as his mother and they can't change that! Jonathan, I have to find a way to get my son back."

"You're not going to be able to do anything until you are back on you're feet mentally and physically. Angela you have to understand this is not going to happen overnight."

"Jonathan I need your help to find a place to go. I don't think Daniel will let me come back home and I can't go to Brads."

"You can stay at my place. I'll be able to help in the evenings and I can have someone out there during the day. It will be the safest and fastest way for you to recover without being alone. I know what kind of fight you are going to have and I will be there for you all the way."

"Thank you. With you and Josh on my side how can I lose!"

I had to stay at the private hospital for several more months before I was moved into a medical rehab center. I stayed there for nearly a year learning how to walk again. Jonathan came to visit me daily to check on my progress. Josh would come by once or twice a week. I finely gave in to Brad and allowed him to visit once a month. The road to recover for us was going to be a long one as well. Ms. Amy started coming by to see me after I allowed Brad to come. She never stayed long and didn't talk much either. Jonathan had everything set up at his house for the day I could move in. I'll never forget when he walked into my room and told me I was being released. I was so excited when he said I was moving out of rehab and into his house. I knew with him I would have a friend to lean on while I recovered.

Angela called Daniel regularly to see if he would bring Danny to see her but he always refused. After a couple of months Daniel would hang up on her. Angela was going to have a long and hard fight ahead of her. Luckily with Jonathan's help she'll get better and will find a way to get her son back, the son she has yet to meet.

The End

Printed in the United States
218140BV00001B/20/P

9 781608 138296